SECRETS & SECOND CHANCES

THE HAPPENSTANCE CHRONICLES · 4

JANICE L. DICK

Tansy & Thistle Press

Secrets & Second Chances

Published by Tansy & Thistle Press, Box 88, Guernsey, Saskatchewan, Canada

Cover by Roseanna White Designs

Map design by Ann-Margret Hovsepian

Interior design by Wild Seas Formatting

Author Photo by Dennis Dick

ISBN (eBook): 978-1-7782026-3-6
ISBN (print): 978-1-7782026-2-9

Endorsements
for the *Happenstance Chronicles*

"The whimsical town of Happenstance and its eccentric characters never fail to delight...A charming story that's the perfect read for a cozy day."
—JOHNNIE ALEXANDER, best-selling & award-winning author of *The Cryptographer's Dilemma* and *The Mischief Thief.*

"Grab yourself a cuppa, and maybe a tasty pastry because you're in for a treat...full of humour and heart in this curious town of second chances. Pure pleasure!"
— ELEANOR BERTIN, author of Lifelines, Pall of Silence, Unbound, Tethered

"The author peopled Happenstance with an array of folksy characters who captivated my imagination and yet were familiar to me...I was plunged into the relationships and carried along through Dick's humour in dialogue and her insightful development of her quirky but believable characters. This redemptive series is a pleasing, entertaining, and joy-filled read."
— DEB ELKINK, award-winning author of *The Third Grace* and *The Red Journal*

"Told with empathy, humor and love, Janice Dick shares her vision of God's grace."
— ROBERTA SOMMERFELD, author of *The Weight of Stones*

"A gentle, light-hearted mystery that affirms the value of community and the hope of second chances. It's always a pleasure to visit the whimsical town of Happenstance."
— JANET SKETCHLEY, author of the *Redemption's Edge* Christian suspense series

Dedication

To anyone who needs a second chance at life

and most especially,
to my dear friend and mentor
—Deanna Robertson—
(March 3, 1937 - September 7, 2023)

ILLUSTRATION BY ANN-MARGRET HOVSEPIAN

Chapter 1

"Remind me again, Abby. Why are you set on going to Ainsworth, Nebraska? What's wrong with Texas? The weather is a lot better there."

Abby glared at Joel in the passenger seat. His hand gripped the armrest, ready to bail if her faded blue Topaz hit a slick spot and slid into the ditch. It bugged her that he didn't trust her driving or her instincts. She didn't trust her instincts anymore either, but she wouldn't tell him that, even as the snow continued to fall, building a dangerous layer of slush on the sides of the road. "I want to see my Aunt Eve. I need a change from Littlefield, and I can't wait tables once Baby comes. I know Eve would welcome me."

"Seems a bit of a risk, seeing as she hasn't answered any of your phone calls to date."

Details! Where was his sense of adventure? "I'll keep trying," said Abby, forcing a smile. "I'd guess she's out on the town with some friends." She wished she believed that. Eve would return her calls if she were able.

"How long since you saw her or even spoke to her, Abby?"

She shrugged, keeping her eyes on the road. "I don't know. A few years." Closer to a dozen. How old would Eve be by now? *Let's see, Mom is fifty-something, I think, and Eve is probably ten years older. Oh wow. She could be over sixty. Is she still alive?*

Joel turned his gaze to her. "What's your Plan B if your aunt doesn't reply? Do we drive all the way to Ainsworth for nothing?"

Abby's stomach tensed. "Joel, I did not force you to come with me. I simply said I was going to Eve's. You're the one who insisted on coming along."

"That's what friends do. Besides, you're nearing the end of your pregnancy." Joel rubbed his forehead with his fingertips, as if a headache threatened. "You know I wouldn't let you drive all the way alone. Even if everything goes well, it's almost a twelve-hour drive." He rubbed at the condensation on his window with his palm. "And this weather doesn't look promising."

"Just a bit of a blow," Abby said, trying to calm herself. Meanwhile, outside the little car, the wind howled, snow pelted the windshield and visibility was decreasing with every mile. She had to hold onto the steering wheel firmly to keep her vehicle on the road. Why couldn't the weather hold out another hour? They were nearing Thedford. Couldn't be far from there to Ainsworth.

As if he'd read her mind, Joel pulled out his phone and tapped his GPS. "The signal is poor with this storm, but from what I can see, there are no direct routes from Thedford to Ainsworth. Either you head north and double back southeast, or you head southeast and then north. Must be lakes in between or something."

"How far?" She caught a flicker of fear in his brown eyes when she chanced a glance his way. He was usually unflappable, but this blizzard was not showing signs of abating. "Assuming all goes well."

He pursed his lips. "About an hour-and-a-half on good roads, but we're not even at Thedford yet. I don't have a clue where that is from here. If there are lakes up there, the roads could get icier too."

Her forceful breath lifted her hair from her forehead. "I could use a bit of encouragement instead of doom and gloom."

"That would be a lie, then, Abigail Maguire, because this storm is bad news."

They were an undetermined distance farther along the number fifteen highway when the car swerved, and Joel involuntarily slammed his foot onto the floorboards. Maybe the lack of a brake on the passenger side was a good thing, as it would almost certainly have resulted in a spin and very probably an accident on this ice. But how could he get the idea through to Abby that she was driving too fast for conditions? He gripped the armrest with stiff fingers and leaned forward, trying to see through the slanting snow. He reached over to turn the output knob to defrost in hopes of relieving the layer of fog on the inside of the windshield.

Even though he knew how Abby would react, Joel formed

his words carefully through clenched teeth. "Abby, if you don't care about my safety or your own, at least consider the life of your baby. He's in your care right now, and you are tempting fate."

She cast him a quick glance. Her forehead glistened with perspiration in spite of the chill in the car. "What do you want me to do? Pull over into the slush? What's that going to help? You think you can do better?"

"No! Not necessarily. But I could take a turn and you could try to relax. All this extra stress could bring the baby on sooner than expected."

"And I could relax while you plow through this blizzard? As if."

"Abby, you're tired. I can hear it in your voice. We know your delivery date is close. Give yourself a break. Let me help."

Her chin lifted beneath her mane of auburn curls. She was so beautiful, so free. These truths both intrigued and frustrated him. Her restless spirit seemed always at war with his careful one. Opposites in many ways. But he'd known that fact as long as he'd known her, and that was almost four years. She was at once vulnerable and independent, afraid but reveling in challenge.

He watched her chin lower and felt her speed decrease. Gradually, to avoid sliding into the ditch, she pulled onto the shoulder of the road, activated her hazard lights and leaned back against the headrest. Her long eyelashes fluttered on her cheeks like butterfly wings, and she looked exhausted. He grabbed the extra blanket he'd tossed into the back seat and attempted to climb out of the vehicle. The wind pushed him so hard he had to use all his strength to open the door. It slammed shut as soon as he was out. His hands on the hood, he struggled around to the driver's side, pulled the door open and threw the blanket around Abby. "Let me help you." He guided her to the passenger side, shielding her as much as possible with his body as the whipping wind and pellets of snow accosted them.

Her passivity now was as frustrating as her pride often was. Sometimes when she gave up, which was a rare thing, it frightened him. Her inner strength was what held her together. On many long-ago days, Abby would have insisted on climbing over the console into the passenger seat, without having to step outside the car, but she was far too cumbersome for that now. Probably another thing that upset her. He pulled open the passenger door and helped her get seated, then moved as quickly as possible to the driver's side.

He scrambled in and pushed his snow-crusted hair back from his face. Rubbing his eyes, he said, "Okay, let's go." He sent Abby a look to see how she was doing, but her eyes were closed. Then he leaned forward to wipe the frost forming inside the windshield again before he put the car into drive. "I won't promise Ainsworth or even Thedford, but I will get us off this forsaken highway to someplace we can wait out the storm." He was surprised at the tension in the steering wheel. Abby had been battling this wild wind for the last three hours.

Her posture straightened. "Good thing this stretch of road is quiet. We could have been hit from behind when we stopped. Never a smart move."

Must you always have the last word? He turned his thoughts to keeping the car on the road and accelerated gently. He'd never been this far north, Texas born and bred with no reason to leave that great state...until now. This was definitely the worst storm he'd ever experienced, and here they were trying to drive in it. Just crazy.

Abby leaned her head back and closed her eyes again. Whatever happened right now, she could do nothing about it. Didn't matter whose idea it was to drive all this way up north. They were here now. Who knew there would be a blizzard? She could imagine Joel's thoughts, "It's winter in Nebraska, darlin'. What did you expect?"

Her hands splayed over her extended middle and she felt Baby move. *Are you frightened, little one? Don't worry, Mama's here. I'll protect you the best I can until you're able to look after yourself. That's life, little guy. You grow up and you're on your own.*

She didn't expect the forlorn feeling that accompanied her thoughts. Almost bitterness, if she were honest with herself. Which she wasn't very good at. She'd been on her own for a couple of years. Through high school, her parents

4

provided a roof over her head and food to eat, but they considered their job done when she graduated and turned eighteen. They were no longer responsible for her well-being, and they never were for Baby's. Not their obligation.

Not one to overthink, Abby considered her current status. Her mother would say, *"Live in the moment, Abigail. That's all you have."*

Now meant a blizzard, a small car that seemed to be getting colder by the minute, and Joel at the wheel. She could rest for a time. But then the questions started: What if she couldn't locate Aunt Eve? What if Baby arrived here in the car, in the middle of this storm? How long would Joel stay with her? As long as Ricky had? Move along when things got complicated?

Abby pulled her hoodie closer around her neck. "Why is it so cold in here? The heater is turned all the way up."

Joel didn't take his eyes off the road, his hands white-knuckled on the steering wheel. "Don't know. Can't check now. Grab another blanket from the back."

With a huff, she tried to reach around to the back seat and, after some scrabbling, managed to snag the corner of a crocheted throw and pull it toward her.

She knew Joel was loyal if anything, otherwise he wouldn't be here. But everyone had a limit to patience, to interrupting their plans. Joel had a future to think of. Whoa! What was wrong with her? She made a point never to worry about the future. It didn't pay. You didn't know how long you had.

But she was facing a reality crisis, as enormous flakes of heavy, wet snow pelted against the windshield. If Baby came now, they'd both be in danger, as surely as she would be soaked and windblown the minute she stepped out of this car. A 1999 model Topaz 4-door did not offer sufficient space to double as a birthing room. And even though Joel helped at the medical crisis clinic, he wasn't experienced or equipped to become her doula.

At that moment, a semi-truck and trailer passed them going in the opposite direction, slapping the car with a layer of slush. Joel said a word he didn't normally use, and slowed. The windshield wipers beat wildly at the offending onslaught, to no avail.

"Keep us on the road, please. Keep us on the road." Joel's mumblings continued as he tried to see through the sleet, and gradually, their field of vision cleared enough to realize they were heading toward the passenger side ditch. Joel eased the steering wheel to the left and kept mumbling. This time it was, "Thank you, thank you, thank you."

"There's a sign," said Joel. "A town up ahead. *Happen-something*. Access one mile."

When the long mile had passed, Joel slowed the car and signaled left. His dutiful habit made Abby snicker. Then giggle. He always kept the rules.

Joel turned left onto the access road and glanced at her for a moment. "What are you laughing at? If that truck had slapped us sightless a minute later, we would have missed the sign and the town."

"I'm sorry." But she couldn't stop her nervous giggles. Add to that her chattering teeth and she lost control. "It's just that you are so predictable. Signaling in the middle of a blizzard when no one can see you."

"That's what integrity is about. Doing the right thing even when no one is watching you."

Her giggling turned to sighs as she wiped her cheeks. She slapped him lightly on the arm. "You are true blue, Joel Pickett."

"And you are punchy. What...what is that?"

"Where?"

"Up ahead."

She squinted into the snow. "It's a..." Before she could figure it out, they were driving through a dark enclosure, momentarily free of wind and snow, with only a dim light in the distance. Whatever it was, she wished it would last all the way into town.

"A covered bridge. I've never driven through one."

Abby braced herself as they exited the bridge. Back to the reality of the storm.

"I'll turn in here," Joel said, pointing to their right. "It's a garage or something." He signaled, and slowly approached the shop.

"The sign says, 'Gas.' We don't need gas."

He sighed. "We do need help. As you stated earlier, our heater is not functioning and we don't know where we are."

"But I don't want to go to Happen-something. I want to go to Ainsworth."

"Why? Your aunt is obviously not there."

She huffed again and folded her arms on top of her belly. "I had a plan. My plan. I was going to Ainsworth. Now you have taken me to Happen-something. I have been hijacked."

He looked at her, wordless, and she clamped her lips shut. Time to back off. For now.

As they glared at each other, there was a tap at the driver's window. Joel lowered the window a fraction to avoid the swirling snow.

A large snowman stood outside and hollered. "Y'all got trouble? I'm gonna open the big door and you drive right on in, okay?"

"Yes, thanks," Joel hollered back.

Abby covered her ears. "You don't have to yell. Baby's getting all upset."

The emotions that flickered through his eyes made her catch her breath. First annoyance, then realization, then fear and determination. And they said guys didn't show emotion. You just had to know how to read it. He was afraid for her, but she'd better curb her whining or he'd leave her alone in this blizzard.

Chapter 2

When the Topaz was fully inside the garage, Gavin Beresford lowered the overhead door and moved back to the driver's window to find out what these people needed. "Where're ya'll from?" he asked, brushing snow off himself.

"Drove up from Texas," said the driver. "Met up with this blizzard."

"Where you headin'? Not great travelin' weather today."

"We figured that out a few hours back, but thought we could still make our destination."

The passenger, a young woman shivering beneath a blanket, leaned forward. "Ainsworth. We're trying to get to my aunt's in Ainsworth. Is it far from here?"

Gavin rubbed his fingers over his five-o'clock shadow. "At least an hour-and-a-half in good weather, ma'am. Best you not try it now. Lotta empty road 'tween here and there."

"We don't have a Plan B," said the young man, stepping out of the car. He reached out a hand to shake, then introduced himself as Joel Pickett.

"Pleased to meet you, Joel. My name's Gavin Beresford, but most ever-body calls me Bear." He glanced into the car.

"That's Abby," said Joel. In a quieter voice he added, "She's going to have a baby."

"Now?" rasped an astonished Bear.

"No. At least, I hope not. But soon. And our heater seems to be malfunctioning. Would you mind if I took a look at it? Nice and dry and warm in here."

"Absolutely. I'll look at it with you. But first," Bear tromped around the car and opened Abby's door. "Excuse me, ma'am. I do believe you need to warm up, and perhaps use the facilities. Follow me."

With some caution in her eyes, the woman cast a glance at Joel to make sure he saw where she was going, then followed Bear into his office.

"Sorry for the mess. My friends keep tellin' me to clean up, but I never get around to it. There's coffee there, made fresh this mornin', and the restroom is down the hall. I should...I think...well, there's more paper and towels under the sink. Help yourself. And then settle on the sofa there until your husband is ready to go."

"Oh, he's not..." She stalled momentarily, then finished with, "Thank you, sir. You're very kind."

He chuckled. "Ain't been called sir in a coon's age. Name's Bear."

Her eyes twinkled at him from behind her tangled mass of red hair. "Thanks, Bear. We appreciate your kindness."

Once Bear and Joel had fixed the heater, which apparently just needed some antifreeze—whatever that was— Abby and Joel proceeded along Bridgeway Avenue, then turned left at the intersection to Main Street North. Abby insisted on driving again, since it was her car. She followed the route around the town square, barely visible through the still-falling snow.

According to Bear's instructions, she saw the sign pointing to the Happenstance Hotel, and chugged along the lane toward the imposing building. Even though the trees lining the road were bare, they offered a degree of shelter from the fierceness of the storm.

Abby was exhausted. She felt shaky and just wanted to check into a room. Maybe it was Bear's coffee. Nasty stuff. Her heart still beat double time, and she apologized silently to Baby.

This change in plans irked her. A lot. But, as Joel tried to make clear to her, a blizzard isn't something you mess with. If offered a warm, dry place to camp, you take it. He reminded her to think of the baby. He never said, "Baby." It was always "the baby."

Abby's mother called her feisty, but right now she possessed only enough adrenaline to force open her car door and climb the steps of the hotel. And there was Joel, at her elbow, guiding her along, her small case in his free hand. As frustrating as he could be at times, she had to admit he was a lifesaver today. Must remember to thank him.

The front door cracked open as they approached, then

opened wide enough for them to enter. A sturdy, elderly woman exclaimed over them while another thinner version waved them inside. Bear had said they were Miss Emmaline and Miss Grayce. He'd said he would call ahead, and the sisters would be expecting them.

"Come into the parlor," said the sturdier one. "We'll worry about the details once you're warm and dry. Follow me."

"Thank you." Abby gratefully trailed the woman to a large room filled with sofas, cozy chairs, occasional tables and large plants. The most welcome sight of all was a fireplace with a roaring blaze that filled every corner of the room with warmth.

"You sit over here, dear," she said, directing Abby to a soft green corduroy couch with several throw pillows piled at one end. "Here's a blanket to tuck around you. You're shaking, my dear. Are you feeling all right?"

"She had some of Bear's coffee to warm up, ma'am. Our heater wasn't working."

"Oh, my dear girl," said the slim sister. "I'm sure Johanna will be here in a minute with..."

Before she could finish her sentence, a robust, red-faced woman appeared with a tray of pastries and coffee. "No caffeine," she said, with a strong German accent. "Not for Baby."

Abby was touched by the care these strangers showed her. More than she'd ever felt back home, except for Joel. He did his best. Abby added cream to the coffee. Smooth and soothing. "This is wonderful. Thank—" but the woman was gone.

"Our Johanna is rather shy. She prefers to serve and leave."

"That is entirely her choice, Emm," said the thin woman. Must be Grayce. "She does a superb job of serving us, and we must respect her personality."

"I wasn't complaining, Graycie, just explaining." She threw up her hands. "Oh, never mind."

Abby closed her lips tightly to suppress the snickers that again tried to force their way out. These two women—the Barlow sisters, said Bear—were an entertaining pair.

Emmaline offered the tray to Joel. "Coffee for you? This

one has caffeine, I believe. Help yourself to the tarts and croissants. I promise you they are the most amazing pastries you have ever consumed."

Abby bit into a warm croissant, lightly dusted with confectioner's sugar, and gasped. "These! Miss Emmaline, these are awesome."

"Yes, indeed." The woman smiled with pride. "We are so blessed to have Johanna with us."

Joel had already consumed a cherry tart, and now took a big bite of his croissant with a similar response. Abby grinned at him, tapping her mouth to signal that he had powdered sugar on his chin. He tapped back, and she reached for her own napkin. Right now she was in the moment, basking in warmth and sweetness and comfort. This was a good time to rest.

She finished her croissant and coffee, snuggled into the cushions and closed her eyes while the others continued to visit. The weather had thrown a wrench into her plans, but this kind of interruption was truly a gift. She would think about tomorrow once it came. Until then...

The next day, the weather pretended nothing had happened. Joel awoke to water pouring from the gutters, and the sun streaming into his upstairs windows. That meant it was late, high time for him to be up. His parents did not condone sleeping in. Ever. Things to do, people to see, souls to save.

He sighed. He knew they meant well, but relief at being out from under their thumb filled him. In his world, relationships were far more important than spouting doctrine. His parents' extreme religious beliefs and lifestyle soured him to religion in general. He believed in God, but his image of the Creator was very different from theirs. Had to be, or he couldn't even think about it any further.

He rolled out of bed and looked out the window. The snow was melting fast in the sunshine, and the birds were enjoying the warmth. The ladies had assigned him this cozy upstairs room when Abby had point-blank told them, "We're not married. I'd like my own room, please."

Their reaction would have been comical if he hadn't been embarrassed for Abby's directness. Shared glances, raised brows, questions longing to be asked. Abby wasn't the most tactful person he'd ever known. She preferred to speak the truth plainly. May as well get everyone on the same page, that was her motto. But sometimes what was honesty to her ended up embarrassing others. But that was Abby. Bold and upfront. He imagined she'd sleep until noon today. Unless this was delivery day. That thought made him weak in the knees.

He'd become used to the idea that Abby was pregnant, but the picture of her actually giving birth and being responsible for a baby frightened him. She was not the responsible type. And babies required constant care, not just when she felt like it. He knew that from experience, with four younger siblings at home. Abby was an only child. The thought almost drove him to prayer.

Abby's parents were what his folks called hippies. Free spirits left over from a past age, people who'd never matured, never grown up, never become part of the fabric of society. Free love without boundaries. It surprised Joel that they had stayed together all these years.

Joel remembered the first day Abby had come to his high school junior class. She'd floated into the classroom, all wispy skirts and filmy blouses and bright scarves tied in her gorgeous hair. The whole room had gone quiet as each person assessed the new girl. She smiled demurely and took her seat with the grace of a butterfly. He'd seen it then, the contrast in her nature. Beautiful, bold, but ready to fly away at a whim.

And then she'd met Ricky and that was the end of Joel's dream. Abby and Ricky were a couple through high school and into college. And Ricky was Joel's best friend. Had been since Ricky and his twin brother Ryley had transferred high schools from California to Texas. But just as tact was not part of Abby's makeup, neither was loyalty part of Ricky's. He ditched Joel like an old shoe, only calling on him when Abby was otherwise occupied. And Joel played his role. Always the pleaser, the peacemaker.

"Enough!" he said, and went to shower and dress. Time to face the new day and all the questions it would hold. The ones that stuck in his head were: What's next? What will we do when Abby realizes Aunt Eve hasn't responded because she probably isn't in Ainsworth anymore?

When Joel reached the dining room where breakfast was served, he was surprised to find Abby already there, visiting with the sisters and a middle-aged man he hadn't met. They all looked up as he entered the room.

"Good morning, sleepyhead." Abby grinned at him from her seat across from Grayce and Emmaline. "You must be making up for yesterday."

"Good morning, everyone. Sorry for being late. That bed was too comfortable."

Grayce spoke up. "Joel, we'd like you to meet our resident school teacher and very good friend, Matthew Sadler. He is a permanent guest here. Matthew, this is Joel Pickett. Did I get that name right, Joel?"

He nodded. "Good to meet you, Matthew."

"You too. And please, call me Matt. I can't get Miss Grayce or Miss Emmaline to comply, but everyone else does."

"Joel," interrupted Emmaline, "do help yourself to Johanna's remarkable breakfast buffet."

"It's amazing food, Joel." Abby pushed herself out of her chair and approached the sideboard for what must be her second helping. "Just another taste or two and I suppose we should be on our way."

"You're still determined to get to Ainsworth? How are you feeling this morning?" Joel couldn't believe Abby felt so well after yesterday's struggle with the steering wheel. "I thought..."

"I know. You thought I'd sleep until noon and be content to stay another day. But no. Time to carry on. I feel excited to be on my way today."

Joel filled a plate and dug into the delicious fare, but it didn't taste as good as it should, dusted with worry as it was. He had serious doubts about Abby's Aunt Eve. He was sure they hadn't spoken in years, much longer than she professed.

"We've been discussing something with Abby this morning." Emmaline's words were a welcome reprieve from his circling thoughts. "We think she should pay a visit to our

Dr. Paula, find out how things are with her baby. She is obviously close to her time."

"I'll be fine." Abby patted her tummy and took a forkful of waffle drenched in syrup and topped with strawberries. "Baby will come when he's ready, which is why I need to get to Ainsworth."

"May I ask what or who is in Ainsworth, dear?" Grayce leveled a gaze at Abby across the sleek oak table. "If your baby makes a sudden appearance, will you be ready? Do you have baby things prepared?"

Abby's fork stilled midway to her next bite. "I, well, I brought a little outfit I used to wear when I was a baby. It was the only thing my mother kept."

"Diapers?"

"No. I'll have to buy a package of disposables. Is there someplace in town I can get them, or should I put that off until we reach Ainsworth?"

Irritation and concern collided in Joel's mind. Abby did not have much money. Her job at the restaurant had brought in enough to pay rent. Thank goodness, her meals were free at work. Was she expecting her aunt to bail her out, support her and the baby? For how long? What was Abby's long-range plan?

He knew the answer to that without further consideration. She had no long-range plan. If he had to, Joel would dip into his own funds, the money he'd been saving for medical school. Abby had no one else.

Joel noted a shared look of alarm between Grayce and Emmaline, and guessed they had also detected Abby's weakness.

He glanced at Matt and thought the guy was doing his best to keep his mouth shut, except for consuming his eggs and toast.

Matt finished his breakfast and stood. "Again, nice to meet you folks, and all the best. I have some more Christmas decorating to do."

"But Matthew, you already put up the decorations from our attic long ago." Grayce looked perplexed.

Matt cleared his throat. "I may have purchased a few new items from Wuppertals' to add some freshness to the display.

This place deserves to shine and celebrate at this time of year."

"How nice." Emmaline twinkled her eyes at Matt. "I trust you completely. But don't forget the nativity scene for the front walk. We want to remind people that Christmas is about Jesus' birth."

"First item on my list. See you all later."

Once Matt had gone, Joel dived back into the situation at hand. "I think going to see the doctor would be a great idea, Abby."

"Don't worry. Besides, I don't want to waste money on unnecessary appointments when everything is fine. I want to use my limited funds wisely."

He ventured farther onto the ledge. "You may be fine, but what about the baby? You need to think about him now, too."

Abby glared at Joel above her glass of orange juice. Before she could shoot him a "mind your own business" comment, Emmaline took a stab at the problem.

"Dr. Paula is stopping by for lunch today, and I'm sure she would give you a quick check right here in your room, dear. Our Dr. Paula is a gem; we've known her all her life. She's a very good physician, just like her father is, and she's also generous."

Joel pieced together the likely scenario. Emmaline planned to request the checkup and pay ahead of time. He doubted their Dr. Paula was as generous with her professional opinions as Emmaline suggested, or even that she had plans to drop by the hotel. Time would tell. Maybe he'd let this play out on its own. He couldn't push Abby any farther than he already had.

Abby snagged Joel as soon as they left the dining room and whispered, "I have another reason we need to move on. The ladies are giving us our rooms out of the goodness of their hearts, but I overheard a phone call earlier this morning. A guy they seem to know well is coming to stay for the holidays, and requested two rooms, starting tomorrow. We need to get out of the way."

"Do you think it's family? No one said anything to me."

"Of course not. They're too polite to ask us to leave, but

Emmaline agreed to have two rooms ready tomorrow. Where are they going to put these guys? Matt uses the third-floor suite, you're on the second floor, and the three other rooms there are under renovation. I have the conservatory, which wasn't a bedroom to start with."

They had reached the quickly converted conservatory, and Abby beckoned him inside. "Come through," said Abby. "The sun is warm on the back deck right now, and the deck chairs are still out there."

The patio doors at the back of the large space opened onto a wood deck, and as Abby said, sunshine warmed the area. They dusted snow off two chairs and relaxed, faces to the sun.

"We need to come to a decision." Abby shifted in her chair to face Joel. "You know I'm determined to go to my aunt's house. It's large, she's always been very sweet when she visited—"

"And when was the last time you saw her?"

Abby felt her irritation rise. "Why? Are you suggesting she has changed personalities since then?"

She saw irritation on Joel's face as well. "No, Abby, I'm strongly suggesting she may not live in that big old house anymore. Have you considered that?"

"But she said she'd stay there forever and we were always welcome."

"Did you ever go see her?"

"Only once. You know my mother, Joel. She never did what she promised, and once she and Dad landed in Texas, she never wanted to leave. I did, however, fly up one Christmas when Aunt Eve sent me a ticket."

"You were how old?"

"It doesn't matter—"

"Abby! Be honest here."

"I was ten, okay? Yeah, it's a while ago. But it was fun and she pampered me, and the house was so dearly dilapidated."

"Dearly dilapidated. That's unique."

"Anyway, I'm going to Ainsworth, with or without you." She quickly added, "I am very thankful you helped me this far, but I don't expect you to take care of me forever. I'm fine on my own. Always have been." She struggled to get out of the angled Adirondack chair and stood. "I'm going to pack my bag and will be ready to leave after lunch. Or sooner."

"Planning to escape the doctor?"

She smirked and wrapped her shawl more tightly against the December chill. "Maybe."

———

Abby returned to her room to pack her bag. Time to hit the road. She wished she could stay to investigate this hotel more thoroughly. She loved old buildings, historic sites that had endured over time, like Aunt Eve's old colonial in Ainsworth, blue-gray with white trim.

According to Grayce and Emmaline, this mansion, formerly known as Barlow Manor, had tunnels beneath it, used in the past for everything from aiding escaping slaves to smuggling alcohol during prohibition.

But today she couldn't delay. She must get to Aunt Eve's before Baby decided to make his appearance. She felt antsy. The idea of an appointment with the doctor was totally unnecessary. Why did these people, and Joel, insist? This was her baby. She would decide. Best to leave before the doctor showed up. But even as she mused on this, the main doors opened and closed, and she heard a new voice in the hall. A female voice. The doctor, she presumed. Abby peeked out into the hallway.

"Good morning, Paula." Matt's voice called from a ladder in the sunroom next to the door.

"Hey Matt. Good to see you. School's out for the season?"

"Yes, ma'am. I'm enjoying the time off, except for the upcoming Christmas pageant."

"I thought the Seligs and their committee had it all cased."

"Yeah, that's what they thought too, but they keep running into snags. Venues already booked, actors suddenly unavailable during the holidays. I've been lending a hand where I can, but I can't play all the parts. Hard to have a pageant without participants."

"Hmm. Too bad. Things will work out, though, I'm sure. Now, where is this new patient?"

Abby tensed, then sighed. May as well face the music and get it over with. She was fine, beyond the restlessness and residual tension from yesterday.

"There she is." Matt descended the ladder and introduced the two women. "I'll leave you to it."

The doctor looked to be in her late thirties, Abby thought, and drop-dead gorgeous, even with her thick, dark hair pulled back into a pony-tail and heavy black glasses sitting on her nose.

Dr. Paula took over, in spite of Abby's determination to lead the interview.

"Let's go to your room. The one beside the conservatory, I'm guessing?"

"Yes, that's where they put me. Nice space. But I need to tell you I feel fine. No reason for you to waste your time with me. Besides, I'm leaving in a few minutes. My bag is all packed."

The doctor ushered her into her room without comment, closed the door behind them and pointed to the unmade bed. "Sit for now. Let's talk."

Abby sat, her grumpy meter climbing at being treated like a child. Even Baby didn't seem to like this doctor, taking the opportunity to kick and squirm.

"When was the last time you saw your doctor?"

Abby bit her lip, having no alternative but to tell the truth. May as well get it out there. "I don't have a doctor. I did a self-test early on, and now I'm obviously pregnant. I've felt fine the whole time."

"No doctor at all? No checkups?"

"That's what I just said."

"Yes, you did. I hoped you were joking. Lie down, please." She opened her black bag and pulled out what she needed.

"I really don't think..."

"Miss Maguire, I have been requested, by several people who care about you, to drop by and make sure everything is on track. Please help me out here. One does not wish to argue with Misses Grayce and Emmaline."

With a great effort, Abby did not roll her eyes. "I'm getting that message."

"They would say, I believe, that your arrival here is not a coincidence, or that I happened to have a free hour this morning."

That was a strange thing to say. Abby hadn't even thought of why or how this all transpired, but she was here now, and ready to move on. It was her nature. A butterfly. Now she had to assuage "the people who cared about her."

"We need to get you to the hospital immediately."

The doctor's words sent Abby into panic mode, an unfamiliar feeling for her. "But I told you, I feel fine. Baby is still moving so he's fine also. Why would I go to the hospital?" She sat up, then stopped at a sharp pain. When she caught her breath, she added. "I am going to Ainsworth today."

"No, I'm afraid you're not. Today you are having a baby."

Of all the nerve. "But I..."

The doctor stared her down. "You are one of those rare women who will have almost no warning of delivery. Your baby will be coming very soon and I'd be much more comfortable having you in the hospital for the event in case I need professional help. It's five minutes away."

"But I...Baby is coming now? Are you sure?"

"I've seen this before," assured Dr. Paula. She pulled out her cellphone and spoke into it. "Get me a delivery room ready stat...I don't care if it hasn't been used in a long time. This can't wait and she won't make it to Athens. We'll be there in five minutes."

She pocketed her phone. "Grab what you need. The ladies have a wheelchair here and I'm going to get it. Wear a jacket. It's pretty outside, but cold."

Stunned, Abby dressed and pulled on her hoodie, the only coat she owned. She reached for her bag and felt another sharp pain. Maybe the doc wasn't kidding. Maybe she knew her stuff. Although Abby was determined to follow her plan, she wouldn't endanger Baby at this stage. She didn't want Joel to deliver him in the back seat of the Topaz. Besides which, Joel had gone to Bear's shop to make sure the heater was working properly. He said he wanted to take a look at the tires as well.

She wished Joel were with her right now. Crazy thought. Abigail Maguire didn't need anyone. She was perfectly fine on her own. She doubled over with the next pain, and once it had passed, allowed Dr. Paula to transfer her to the wheelchair and out to a waiting ambulance. Wow, they worked fast out here. Who'd have guessed? Doctor Paula must have clout.

So much for getting to Ainsworth.

Chapter 3

Joel had just finished checking the heater when his phone buzzed. Abby. Why would she call him? Did she need help with something? She hated to ask anyone for help. Maybe she was letting him know to bring her car back, and then she could leave. *Oh, Abby, stop and reconsider!* He tapped the button and answered. And almost dropped the phone.

"Joel, it's me. I'm in the hospital. Dr. Paula insisted on checking me over and said...ow, ow, ow..."

"Abby? Abby, are you okay?"

After a long silence, she was back, panting. "Sorry. Baby is on the way. I'm fine, but I wish you were here. Can you get away?"

"Of course. But Abby, I'm not...do you want me right there with you?"

"Get over it, Joel. I need you to talk me through this. Besides, if you're going to be a doctor, you'll need some practice."

"I haven't had any training yet. I'm not familiar with deliveries." He heaved a sigh. "I'll be right there."

"You okay, buddy?" Bear hovered nearby, his hat backwards on his head. "If that was your wife callin', you better hustle on over."

"She's not..." He hesitated. "She's not my wife."

"Your girl, then. I ain't gonna judge you."

"You don't understand. We're not even...how do I explain this? We're not a couple. It's not even my baby."

"Now you got my attention. Get on out to my truck and keep talkin'."

Joel caught the knit cap Bear tossed in his direction and tugged it low over his ears. The sun shone brightly outside, but the air had a bite to it. "She was involved with one of my best friends. At least he used to be my friend, but when he found out she was pregnant, he said adios and took off. To Europe. Far away."

They climbed into the cab of the old but pristine half-ton truck. "Why are you here, with her?"

Why, indeed? Because she had no one else who would help her? Because they were friends?

He slammed the door behind him. "Because I love her."

"And what's her take on that?"

"She's so blasted independent she won't let herself consider it."

"Whoa! That's a load to carry." The big-hearted man he'd known for about twelve hours reached over and squeezed his shoulder. Joel's heart was in his throat, his mind raced, fear and hope vied for top place. Abby had called. She wanted him with her. He would stuff his discomfort inside and help her. This time, a prayer escaped his lips. A short one. "God?"

"He's got ya, kid. Don't worry. You got friends here too."

***

Joel's experience at the hospital was surreal. Dr. Paula proved as competent as he expected, and the nurses who assisted her showed concern and understanding for both him and Abby.

They hovered around the patient, calming her and easing her discomfort, but throughout, Abby held Joel's hand with one of hers in a knuckle-crushing grip. Mentally, he filed everything he observed with what he'd have to learn in medical school. Personal experience was the best teacher, and this was as personal for him as it was for Abby.

However, Joel was an emotional wreck. He forced himself to project calm and confidence, but he winced at Abby's every cry, and stood in shock when the doctor held up a real live baby. How could a person lose their sense of reality like this? Abby now had a responsibility to a tiny, helpless human being. God help them all.

When Abby dropped his hand to claim her baby—a girl, in spite of her assertion it would be a boy—Joel slipped out of the delivery room to splash cold water on his face and stare at himself in the bathroom mirror. In the past two weeks, his life had shifted into an alternate reality. How did a young, unattached male from Texas, with his sights set on medical school, end up in a hospital washroom in northwest Nebraska, in a tiny town called Happenstance?

Abby lived with a no-strings-attached attitude, but Joel

couldn't deny there were strings. Lots of them. All tangled and knotted, some strong, some frayed. He walked the short hallway of the hospital's second floor until he thought he might wear a path into the 1940s heavy-duty linoleum.

Eventually, Dr. Paula caught up with him. "How are you doing? Bear tells me you are the proverbial Good Samaritan. Thanks for helping your friend through this."

"She doesn't have anyone else to lean on."

"Yeah, but not just anyone would give up what you did to stick with her. You're remarkable."

"Not really," replied Joel. "I'm a mess. This giving birth is a life-changing event, and I'm only a bystander."

The doctor held his eyes. "I think you're more than that, but I'll let you work that through. Right now, I suggest you hunt up some good coffee, have yourself a talk with someone like Bear—oh, and don't drink his coffee; I'm off duty now—and try to relax. Abby will need you tomorrow, even if she won't admit it."

"Thanks, Doc. I think I'll do that." Joel wondered how the doctor had figured out that much about them in such a short time. He vaguely remembered Bear having a brief but serious conversation with Dr. Paula when he brought Joel to the hospital. In this town, people got to know you, whether you wanted them to or not. He welcomed the freedom to be who he was, to speak his mind, at least to Bear, and to know others had his back. It was all pretty crazy, in a good way.

Abby, weary but excited, was back at the hotel before lunch the next day, seeing as she and Baby Girl were both doing well. Dr. Paula promised to drop by to check on her when she came for dinner later that day.

When Grayce and Emmaline asked her for permission to invite a few people for dinner with Dr. Paula, Abby was surprised. "Of course, you can have a dinner party. This is your hotel." She also knew they were expecting their two new guests, but they had said nothing about it. At this moment, she was simply too tired to move anywhere else.

"Yes dear, we know," said Grayce, "but as you are still recovering from childbirth, we didn't wish to upset you by inviting too many strangers for you to meet."

"Or," suggested Emmaline, "we could have your dinner brought to your room."

Abby stood to pick up a whimpering Baby Girl from her bassinet nearby and hugged her to her chest. A hand-carved baby bed had been brought down from the attic, and the thought flitted through Abby's mind that neither of the Barlow sisters had children. Maybe they themselves had used this bed, although it didn't look *that* old.

"I'll be fine to join you for dinner. I feel wonderful and excited and...maternal!" Her eyes widened as she said this to the Barlows. "I'll have a good, long nap, and maybe by then I can settle on a name and introduce Baby Girl properly."

Abby had not asked Joel for his input on Baby's name. She saw no need to involve him. This was her responsibility.

She and Baby Girl had a nap, and she was finally awakened by voices. Unfamiliar ones. Funny how she knew the timbre of the personalities she'd already met: Miss Grayce, Miss Emmaline, Matt, Dr. Paula, Bear, Johanna. But these voices differed. They sounded old. Joel would chide her for that word choice. Okay then, mature. Two people, man and woman. The woman spoke with an accent, German, like Johanna, but with a more extensive use of words.

Abby threw back the light blanket she had pulled over herself earlier and gently placed her sleeping baby into the bassinet. Her little girl had a head of thick, dark hair—compliments of Ricky—and a sweet rosebud mouth. Abby felt something she'd never felt before. A connection. A belonging. A bond. Even though she knew her parents loved her in their way, they didn't have a strong bond with her. Free and easy, that was their mantra. She'd tried to emulate that, to stay unencumbered and uncommitted, and thought she'd succeeded, but it wasn't enough. This child before her was a miracle. First, she wasn't. Then she was.

Abby wasn't accustomed to musings, other than what to wear or how to apply her makeup in an artistic fashion. With a head shake, she pulled on a dark elastic-waist skirt and a cozy, aqua-colored sweater with pockets. Her strength had returned, except for a few shivers that visited now and then, possibly from the shock of giving birth. She couldn't process it all now.

At that moment, Baby Girl shuddered in her sleep, and Abby's heart softened with love like she'd never known. She tucked the tiny quilt around the sleeping infant and lightly stroked her head. "Rest easy, darling. Mama's here."

A light knock at her door drew her out into the hall. As she greeted Dr. Paula with a smile, the aroma of seasoned poultry wafted through the hallway. She closed her eyes and inhaled.

"Heady, isn't it?" Dr. Paula watched her. "You look well, but don't overdo. Come back and lie down when you're tired."

Abby glanced back into her room. "It smells heavenly, but I can't leave Baby Girl alone."

"I come bearing gifts." Dr. Paula handed her a box with a picture of a small intercom. "It's a baby monitor. Maisie, our local hairdresser, sent it over."

They set it up on the dresser next to the bassinet, and after some assurances from the doctor, Abby nodded and left, knowing she'd have to trust this simple device.

As the two approached the dining room, the lilt of voices met them. Matt held a chair for a tiny elderly woman with a cloud of white hair. The sisters were already seated, and looked up with matching smiles. As different as they were from each other, the familial similarities could not be denied.

"Abby," said Grayce. "Splendid that you could come for dinner. You look rested."

"Yes, dear," added Emmaline, who always had words to share. "You look fabulous for what you've gone through. Not that I would know, never having had children of my own, but..."

"Shush, dear," Grayce whispered in Emmaline's direction. "It is unhelpful to speak of things with which you have no experience."

"Why ever not? If we only spoke of things we knew, we'd hardly speak at all."

Grayce smiled and lifted her chin. "Yes, quite."

"Fiddle." Emmaline continued, undeterred, and turned back to Abby. "I say you look like you weathered that particular storm well enough. Please, do have a seat. Matthew will assist you."

Matt took his role seriously, seating her and Dr. Paula, then introducing them to the guests. "This is Reverend and Mrs. Selig. They live in the parsonage right beside Our Redeemer Community Church. You may have seen it on your way into town, at the intersection of Bridgeway and Main."

"Hello to you both." Abby reached out to clasp hands with each of them. "I'll have to take your word for it, Matt. We arrived in the middle of the blizzard, and were thankful to see a few feet in front of us."

Joel entered the room and took the remaining chair. "Straight to this lovely hotel, where we were welcomed like long lost family." He nodded to the Barlow sisters. "We are thankful." He looked expectantly at Abby.

"Yes," she said. "We are grateful to all of you for taking us in and helping us through this new experience."

Mrs. Selig asked Abby a few questions in her accented English, also commenting on how soon she had returned to the hotel after the birth. "When we had our little girl, I stayed ten days in hospital, and then my Otto, he has to care for us and to cook, but we survived. Those were different times." The old woman's eyes looked sad.

Abby shuddered. "I can't imagine having to stay in bed that long. I'd go crazy."

"Yes, things have changed over the years," said Paula. "We now know the body gains strength through carrying on with normal routines as soon as possible. Of course, there are exceptions, but in your case, Abby, you're young and healthy, and with a bit of rest, you'll be back to normal very soon."

"As normal as adding a baby to your life allows!" Abby smiled as she thought of her baby. What a sweet addition to normal.

Conversation slowed considerably when Johanna served the roast chicken with baked apples, roasted fingerling potatoes and tiny carrots. Abby noticed that although everything tasted excellent, with the perfect blend of spices, Johanna had been easy on seasonings. The doctor had suggested Abby stay away from any foods that might bother hers or Baby's stomach. This was a new consideration for Abby, who had always eaten anything she wanted without repercussions.

Matt broke into her thoughts, asking if she had named her baby yet. Joel darted a look at her as well, looking excited to hear her decision, if she had made one.

"I'm happy to say I have arrived at the ideal name for Baby Girl. Since Christmas is only ten days away, I've decided to call her Noelle."

"That's perfect," chorused the guests.

Abby slanted a glance at Joel. He caught her eye and smiled, giving her a slight nod of affirmation. Not that she needed anyone to approve of that name, but she was happy Joel liked her choice. There were many things they disagreed on. The thought brought back her determination to remain independent. Life was an adventure, and now she had Noelle to share hers.

The conversation around the table shifted to the Christmas pageant, a town-wide event that was swiftly approaching. "A committee was struck back in September to oversee the process," said Reverend Selig. "It's our job to make sure it all comes together."

"We all need to do our part," said Matt. "I don't want you to have to handle all the stress, what with people unable to follow through on their commitments."

"Thank you, Matt," said Reverend Selig. "We thought it was all sewed up, but circumstances change, and some of the participants have had to opt out."

"I understand everyone is busy, it's Christmas," replied Matt, "but we've already put a lot of work into the whole event."

Their discussion piqued Abby's interest. "What kind of pageant are you presenting? Is it the usual Christmas carols at the church with a manger scene? Sounds fairly simple."

Matt grinned and shook his head. "No, this is a far more detailed endeavor. It's a living nativity. The plan is to have actors all over town dressed up as the people of Bethlehem."

"Yes," continued Mrs. Selig. "There will be, in the field shepherds, and angels that sing over them, and a village scene with a—how do you call that, Otto, where they keep animals?"

"The stable, my dear. And farriers making horseshoes, and silk sellers, fish sellers, leather makers, spice merchants. All these little shops must be set up in and around

Happenstance to make the place look authentic."

His wife took over the explanations again. "People drive around in their cars with maps to tell them where to go, and they see all these things. And music and lights. Wonderful it will be. We have even our own Mary and Joseph with their baby, born a month past."

Paula checked her wristwatch. "I'm sorry, but I have to run. It's been great to be here, ladies." She rose and kissed Grayce and Emmaline. "This old place holds many special memories for me." She turned to Abby as she pushed her chair back. In a low voice, she suggested, "It might be a good time to rest up now. Too much interaction may keep you awake, and Baby—Noelle—will be needing you."

"I think you're right." Abby hadn't realized she was so tired. The evening had been interesting and she was glad she'd come out to mix for a while. "Thanks again for everything."

When Abby returned to her room, a cup of steaming tea waited on her night table. How did Johanna get from the kitchen to the conservatory without any of them seeing her? That was one mystery she didn't have energy to solve right now.

Noelle still slept, while Abby enjoyed the tea and readied herself for bed. No sooner had she relaxed beneath the covers than Noelle awoke hungry and in need of a diaper change. It was up to her now, Abby knew. This new, unfamiliar phase of life would test her strength, but she was sure she was up to it. She had to admit though, she was thankful to still be at the hotel in Happenstance, instead of on the way to Ainsworth, or in a strange town with no place to stay.

She wondered when Joel would head back home. The thought of not having him around was hard for her to imagine, if she were honest, but she dismissed it from her mind as she lifted sweet Noelle from the bassinet.

Chapter 4

Joel enjoyed the rest of the conversation around the dining table. The hotel felt more like a home than a temporary place to stay. Shortly after Abby returned to her room, the Seligs left as well, and not long after, the doorbell chimed and the door opened without waiting for anyone to answer it.

Emmaline popped up. "It must be Sandy and his protégé." She moved toward the hallway, followed closely by Grayce.

Matt grinned from ear to ear, directing his words toward Joel. "This guy, Sandy—officially Lysander Patrick Joseph Fitzpatrick III—is a treasure. Wait till you meet him!"

"That's a moniker and a half! And his companion?"

"Never met him. Part of Sandy's work, I think. He called him Cal. We'll know in a minute." Matt stood to join the welcome party, and Joel followed.

A tall, wiry man with the strongest Irish brogue Joel had ever heard was already telling stories, tall tales by the sound of it, and his sidekick, a slip of a woman with short crimson hair sticking out in all directions, entered with their suitcases. Surely this wasn't Cal. Joel wondered why Sandy didn't carry the luggage. He was lean, but certainly larger than the woman. Maybe it gave her something to do. She didn't look like she loved introductions to new people.

"This be Cal." Sandy jerked his thumb toward the newcomer. "My right-hand person, so to speak. Helps me with the project I've undertaken for me teaching handbook, and adds to her own thesis preparation as she goes. Very dependable."

Cal bobbed her head toward the group, no smile, her nose ring and rows of eyebrow- and earrings glistening in the light. "Nice place. Where do you want these bags?"

Sandy threw his head back and laughed. "She has a vast vocabulary, but chooses her words succinctly." His laugh was infectious and Joel couldn't help joining in. Sandy obviously loved all the attention he could get. Cal did not even break a smile.

Joel shot a glance at the Barlow sisters, whose eyebrows had risen high enough to nearly disappear into their hairlines. They were sending silent messages back and forth with wide eyes.

Finally, Grayce spoke, eyebrows relaxing a degree. "Do come into the parlor, everyone. I'm sure Johanna has some refreshments to bolster us before we turn in for the night."

"Yes," agreed Emmaline. "We have a full house right now, but we will make do—"

"I don't need a room," interrupted Cal. "I have my bedroll. Any space on the floor is sufficient."

"Oh no! We couldn't let you do that." Emmaline turned her questioning gaze to Grayce. Joel could almost hear her thoughts. *What are we going to do? They can't bunk together.*

After a moment's consideration, Grayce spoke. "My sister and I can share a room, Miss Cal, so you will have decent accommodation. And Sandy will surely be fine for now in one of the rooms being renovated. Matt, will you please call one of the Wuppertal girls to tidy a room?"

"I'm on it." Matt pulled out his phone and texted a few words.

"Don't change your rooms around for me. I can sleep in any corner. And my name is just Cal."

"Yes, of course." Miss Emmaline did not look convinced.

"The chapel!" Grayce smiled at her solution. "Matthew, would you please show her to the chapel?"

He nodded. "Follow me, Cal."

The woman picked up her bedroll and a small duffle and pushed forward toward Matt without meeting the eyes of anyone there. Matt led her to the end of the hallway, then turned left in the direction of the chapel.

"So be it," said Grayce.

"Brilliant!" Sandy winked at the Barlow sisters. "Do not worry about Cal. She's resilient, from what I've seen. You will barely notice her presence."

Joel could see the sisters weren't persuaded, but this wasn't his circus. He turned to go up to his room, just as a smiling teenage girl knocked on the door and joined them from outside. They called her Leah, and as she carried a mop and bucket, he assumed this was "one of the Wuppertals" who came to the ladies' rescue when they needed a cleaning lady or chambermaid. Talk about instant service.

"I'll have a room ready in about half an hour," she said with a smile. "Go enjoy a cup of tea and by then I'll be done."

"Dear girl," sighed Grayce, patting her shoulder. "You are certainly a lifesaver."

"No problem at all," she assured them. "I needed a break from studying chemistry anyway."

Instead of following Leah upstairs, Joel opted to join the group for "a cuppa before bed," as Sandy called it. He was fascinated by this Irishman everyone seemed to know, the "quirky wood sprite," as Matt dubbed him. Joel couldn't pass up on an opportunity to listen to fantastical tales from a master storyteller.

Cal did not reappear that evening, no surprise to Joel. Perhaps she got her fill of Sandy when they worked together. Although an excellent weaver of tales, he could eventually become overwhelming, especially if you were an introvert.

Abby ventured out of her room the next morning to the sound of voices from the dining room. Laughter and exclamations and the aroma of fresh coffee. When she reached the room, it seemed overfull, and she stood a minute to gather her thoughts. Who were all these people? Oh yes, the two guests, added to an already full house. *My fault. I need to move out. But to where?*

"Ah, Abby." Matt beckoned her forward, then stood to introduce her. "Friends, Irish, country folk, this is Abby Maguire, temporarily stopped here by the delivery of her first child, Noelle, who must still be asleep. Abby, this is Lysander Patrick Joseph Fitzpatrick the Third—"

"My name be Sandy and that's enough, Matthew. Ma'am." He nodded and beamed a smile in her direction. "We be pleased to meet you. Will we be graced to see the littlest princess too?"

"Of course," assured Abby. "We are two for one right now."

"Sandy, your brogue has deepened over the last few years. What happened?" Matt asked.

"I spent much of me time in the good land across the pond," Sandy said.

"He puts on the dog for attention." This curt statement came from the other new guest.

"Forgive me," said Matt. "This is Sandy's cohort, Cal."

"Hello, Cal." Abby eyed the other woman. Her spiked red hair looked like porcupine quills, and if you added in the piercings and tattoos, she looked like a small but formidable foe. A bit like a ferret. Besides her brilliant hair color and the metal in her face and ears, tattooed leaves vined their way up her arm and coiled around her neck. Abby gulped, her smile a grimace. *Am I getting old? Why does this bother me? I have tatts and piercings too, but that vine is going to choke her— or me.* Maybe it was the whole enchilada that hit her full force.

Cal nodded in her direction, a knowing glint in her large green eyes. She offered no words of greeting at all.

That was fine with Abby. She had nothing in common with this woman, besides a bent for eccentricity. Abby caught a flicker of humor in Joel's eyes. She wrinkled her nose at him and poured herself a cup of Johanna's superb coffee, complete with a generous addition of cream. This mothering made her hungry.

Abby had barely begun to eat when she heard whimpering on the monitor she had set beside her. She rose and left to check on Noelle. If not for the sweet offerings in the dining room, she would have stayed in her room with her little girl. Who needed dagger-sharp looks from a stranger she had no connection with. But her own hunger drew her back, after she had tended to Noelle and fed her.

Back in the dining room, everyone oohed and aahed over Noelle, as she expected they would. Cal, however, made no comment, ignoring the sentimental attitude around her. Instead, she seemed to cringe and move away from the baby. Abby could understand, to a point. She'd never been a baby-person herself in her younger years, maybe because she was too self absorbed. But surely even this brazen young woman could see how beautiful Noelle was.

Her thoughts were interrupted by Emmaline, who had left the room to answer the telephone. This hotel still had a landline. High time for some updating.

Emmaline stood in the doorway, looking directly at her. "Call for you, Abby."

"For me?" Who would be calling her? Aunt Eve, finally? She had pretty well given up on hearing from her aunt. She handed Noelle to Joel and hurried to take the call. The voice that answered identified herself as Mrs. Selig, the pastor's wife.

"My dear Abigail," she began, "my husband and I, we have been talking together, and we were asking each other, would this young woman and her new baby want maybe to have a place more long-time to stay. And we said, yes, she might. I am asking you."

"It's kind of you to be concerned," said Abby. "What were you thinking of? There are no other hotels in town."

"Well, at our place, that is what I am saying," replied Mrs. Selig. "We have here rooms more than we use. You think on it and then telephone back to us, yes?"

"Oh. You have...may I...give me a bit of time to think about this. And thank you very much, Mrs. Selig."

"Yes, you are welcome."

The older woman hung up, leaving Abby surprised and unsure. Yes, she would love a place to stay so the Barlow sisters could have their hotel back, and right now, there were too many strangers here. Cal gave her the creeps. But would the Seligs' residence be the right place for her?

But how long am I staying in Happenstance? She had planned to head out soon to Aunt Eve's, if she could ever establish contact. It didn't pay to move at this point. But how to tell Mrs. Selig, who had offered her a place to stay? It sounded like more long-term than she needed. Right now, her whole world was in upheaval.

Joel was at her elbow. "What's up, Abby? Did your aunt finally get in touch with you?"

"No." She told him her story and he listened intently.

"Maybe you should accept the Seligs' offer, at least until we figure out our next steps."

"You mean my next steps. You are not required to stay by my side, Joel. You have no commitment to me."

His eyes conveyed a message she could not read, or maybe would not acknowledge. They'd never been more than friends. Had they? Why did he insist on taking care of her?

"Until you get settled either here or in Ainsworth with Noelle, I'm here for you, Abby."

Okay. She thinned her lips and nodded her thanks. She would accept, for now, because although she wouldn't admit it to anyone, she appreciated his help and his company, and he knew her background. She could do it alone, of course, as she always had done, but now she had Noelle, and no clue how to take care of her. And why not accept Joel's help and let him feel useful? That way, she'd get more sleep and be back on her feet sooner.

Chapter 5

"I need to go to Ainsworth now," said Abby. She sat at the hotel dining table, her phone in her hand, staring at a Google map. Lunch was done and Johanna had cleared the table, but Abby, Joel and the Barlows still sat finishing cups of tea. "You people aren't listening to me. I've tried finding my aunt, unsuccessfully, but I'm sure I can locate her once I'm there. I remember the big, old house where she lives."

She saw Joel take a deep breath and knew he expected her to go snarky at any suggestion he might make. But she determined to hold it in. Let him have his say.

"Abby, why don't you give Noelle a few days to get settled? How are you going to manage her in the car?"

"I'll just stop on the side of the road or at a service station to change and feed her."

"Do you have a car seat?" asked Emmaline.

"A car seat? I'll just hold her."

"While you're driving?" Joel popped up from his chair.

Uh oh. He was upset. That didn't happen often and she wasn't sure how to handle it.

"Surely you know there's a federal law about car seats, Abby. Insurance. Accidents. All that. You can't ignore the law."

"You're too caught up in keeping rules—"

"My dear girl," interrupted Grayce. "Children are protected by the law, and if you don't keep that law, your little girl may be taken away from you."

That shook Abby. No one, absolutely no one, would take her daughter away from her. She searched her mind for ideas. "Where do I get one of those things? Is there a second-hand store here in Happenstance?"

"They're pretty strict about the guidelines for use," said Joel. "I looked it up. The seat has to pass certain tests. How about I run into Athens and see if I can find one?"

"Good idea. I'll go with..." Abby cleared her throat. "Noelle and I will wait here. We appreciate your offer."

"May I use your car?"

"Of course. How else would you get there?"

———— ✿ ————

Once Joel left, Abby went to her room and lay on her bed, pulling the bassinet close enough to stroke Noelle's soft hair as she slept.

No option but to think ahead. She couldn't leave whenever she wanted to anymore. She was...she didn't want to say stuck, but that's how it felt. She wouldn't leave her baby for anything, but she hadn't counted on being literally grounded. She hadn't counted on having her wings clipped. That was hard on a butterfly.

What now? Could she make it to Ainsworth on her own, she and Noelle? The more she thought about it, the less she wanted to drag Joel around with her. Not that she had forced him to come along in the first place, but what would he do once they got to Ainsworth? He'd have to find an airport and fly back home. Spend more of his savings because of her.

Thing is, she didn't have enough money to pay Bear for fixing the heater, besides buying a baby chair or whatever, plus gas to get to Aunt Eve's.

Where was her aunt, anyway? Abby had been too distracted lately with Noelle and Joel and all that was happening to think about how to find Aunt Eve. How could the woman up and leave just when Abby needed her? Especially now, when Abby finally decided to take her up on her open invitation. But, she was determined not to call her mom, not even to ask her about Eve. Her mom didn't even know where her only child was, never mind a sister distanced by time and miles. *"Happy adventures,"* Mom had called when Abby left home after college. End of a chapter. No help there.

That was the problem. Abby did not like to ask for help. She had always been self reliant, even when she found out she was pregnant. But now, everything had changed. She had a helpless little person to look after, to protect. And she didn't have a clue how to do it. She didn't know who to talk to. Dr. Paula was kind but she had other patients to see to. The Barlows were concerned and compassionate, but she wasn't their problem, and they had a houseful of guests.

After dinner last night, the Seligs had offered to help her, but they were old. What would they know? What could they do?

Abby sat up in bed, her back against the wall. There had to be a way to figure this out. For the first time in a long while, she needed a plan. A safe plan. The truth hit her like a sudden gust of wind. She could not drag Noelle to Ainsworth without having a place to stay. They could not afford a hotel. If her aunt had gone away for an extended holiday or something, they would have nowhere to go. Stranded in northern Nebraska.

Just then she heard a quiet knock on her door. She crawled off the bed and slipped into the hallway. Joel was back, a tentative smile on his face.

"Come sit in the parlor where we can talk." He kept his voice to a whisper, glancing at Noelle, which Abby found endearing.

"Hang on while I grab the monitor."

They settled on one of the cozy couches while Joel updated her. "First, I could not find any used car seats. Apparently, the rules are strict. You can't use a second-hand seat unless it's inspected, and that costs money. The new ones are pricey. I'm not sure what else I can do about that right now. And we can't leave here in your car without a seat for Noelle."

"No, not if it endangers her, or...you know...if they would take her." Abby couldn't face that thought. It made her shudder to think of it.

Joel patted her shoulder. "We would never let it come to that. We'll figure it out somehow."

"We?"

"Yes, we. I'm not ditching you like—sorry. Didn't want to bring that up."

"You're right, Joel. Like Ricky did. It's his loss."

"You got that right. There's something else, Abby."

"Of course. Shoot."

"I have an idea for locating your aunt. You interested?"

"Of course, I'm interested. I've been racking my brain here."

Joel leaned toward her, grabbing her hand. "Dr. Paula

used to be a cop—"

"No way! Huh! She does have a commanding presence."

"Yeah, so she has connections on the force. There's this Constable Rising Moon who is reportedly good at finding missing persons. She may be willing to look for your Aunt Eve if we ask her to."

Abby leaned back, pulling her hand away. She didn't mind so much asking help of a stranger. "Okay. Let's do it. I mean, yes, I would like Constable Rising Moon to find my aunt. Obviously, I'm not having any luck myself."

"Great. I'll call her." Joel grabbed his phone. "I got her contact information from Dr. Paula."

He rose to leave the room, then stopped to ask, "What's Eve's last name?"

"Um...let me think. Tanner...no, Turner. Not sure, but that sounds right."

The baby monitor picked up some squeaking sounds and Joel offered to check on Noelle. Hesitantly, Abby agreed. She felt tired, now that a plan was being made. She'd lean back and close her eyes for a moment. Joel was an eldest sibling; he knew how to hold a baby.

Abby woke to a feeling of warmth and whispers. Gradually squinting her eyes open, she realized she had fallen asleep. A blanket covered her, and she lay on a cushion. Without moving her head, she looked across to another couch to see Joel holding Noelle on his lap, talking to her ever so softly. Her dark eyes were on his, as if she understood every word.

His gaze on her baby was one of love, of wonder. As she observed them, she felt a pull toward him, toward them. It was like a family. How would that feel? Could she ever let herself consider an arrangement like that?

Then he became aware that he was being watched, and raised his gaze to Abby's. His eyes, first deep pools of warmth, suddenly dimmed, and he cleared his throat as if he were coming out of a dream. "Hi Abby. We were getting acquainted, Noelle and I. By the way, I love the name you settled on. Did you have a lot of other possibilities?"

Abby pushed herself to a sitting position and pulled the blanket up around her. "Oh yeah. I'll run a few by you. Stormy, since she arrived right after the storm that brought us here. Or Skye, because her face is as beautiful as a fresh spring sky." She pulled a bit of paper from the pocket of her sweater and read. "Aria, Lilith, Aurora, Orianna, Seraphina, Oona, Luna, Willow, Pixie, Posy." She paused to look at Joel. "You okay?"

He gave his head a shake. "Yeah, sure. I didn't realize what a difference a name could make. Whatever you call her, it brings something along with it."

"I still need a second name. Any you prefer?"

"You're asking me?"

"I just did. Not that your preference will sway me from making my own final decision, but some feedback would be helpful."

"I'm a little afraid if I say I hate one of those names, you'll pick it."

She laughed. "I'm not that contrary, am I? Wait, don't answer that."

He sighed as he raised Noelle to his shoulder, where she snuggled into his neck. He patted her back as he rose and slowly paced with her. "Okay. You're definitely aiming for something different than the usual. Not surprising. I think my favorite of the ones you mentioned is Aria."

"What names came to your mind before I mentioned these?" she asked, wondering what he had expected.

He stared at her as if to gauge her reaction before he answered. He pulled his phone out of his back pocket and thumbed through it. Then he cleared his throat and read, "Anna, Lily, Jane, Phoebe. But then I thought of who her mother is and got a few more exotic ideas. Butterfly, Wren, Chloe, Ember, Lyric."

She didn't know what to say. The last few were catchy. They seemed to fit. "I like those. Wren and Ember and Chloe. What was the other one? Lyric. That's cool."

"Not Butterfly?"

"Do you like that one?"

He thinned his lips. "Not for her. It's more for you."

She stilled. He never talked this way to her. Maybe having a baby in his arms gave him the boldness to be open with her.

39

She knew she mattered to him, otherwise why would he have put his life on hold to accompany her all the way to Nebraska? But this Joel seemed different. She had to end this before he lost himself.

She rose and took Noelle from him. "Well, that was an interesting discussion. I'll let you know what I decide. And it won't be Butterfly."

Joel felt bereft when Abby took Noelle from him. He'd better pull himself together. Abby wasn't his, and neither was her little girl. Maybe they never would be. He scrubbed his hands over his face and stood, wondering what to do next. At that moment, Johanna appeared with a cup of coffee. She set it on the end table next to where he'd been sitting, along with a still warm cinnamon roll, nodded to him, and left.

He sat again, glanced at his watch and saw it was mid-afternoon. He ate the amazing roll. The hot, strong coffee soothed him and brought him back to reality.

He carried his cup and plate to the little table that sat outside the kitchen and left it there for Johanna. Then he paced the hall as he made his call. It took a while to get an answer.

"Constable Rising Moon here. Who's calling?"

"Um, hi, Constable Rising Moon. This is Joel Pickett. I got your contact information from Dr. Paula. She—"

"You're the people staying at the Happ Hotel, right? She said you needed help in a missing persons case."

"Kind of. My friend was headed to Ainsworth to find her aunt, Eve Turner. She's not sure of the last name. We haven't been able to reach her at all, and Abby, my friend, is desperate to locate her. The doctor said you might be able to help."

"Yeah, sure. I owe her one. More than one. And I have a few minutes. I'll put out a call now. Eve Turner? Ainsworth? Approximate age?"

"Uh, not sure, but I'm thinking maybe sixties?"

"Got it. I'll get back to you when I find something."

"Hey, thanks a lot. Appreciate it."

"Any friend of Paula's..."

She hung up and Joel slipped the phone into his pocket.

He felt antsy. Maybe he'd hike up to Bear's and see what he was up to. He didn't want any more coffee, so he wouldn't be threatened by a cup of Bear's poison.

Cal stepped back into the shadows as Joel left the room, car keys jingling in his hand. At least he was smart enough to look for a solution. What a mess they'd gotten themselves into. The young mother had no idea how to care for her child. And no car seat? What was she thinking? Likely, she wasn't. Hadn't thought about anyone but herself all her life.

You could tell by her flowing clothes, thought Cal as she re-entered the chapel. *A mother doesn't dress like that, too many things to catch scarves and large sleeves on, especially when carrying a baby. Anyone knew that. Abby was obviously unprepared to be a mother. Poor little baby, such a sad state to be in. Must watch out for her.*

Cal pulled on her jacket and wrapped a scarf around her neck. Knit cap and mittens in hand, she set off for the great outdoors. As she passed the dining room, she saw a note on the table. Addressed to her. "For Cal. Coffee to warm you."

She glanced up at the kitchen door but heard no sound from within. Too weird. But the coffee looked inviting, and when she sniffed it, she inhaled the rich hazelnut aroma with pleasure. She wrapped her hands around the sleeve on the cup and let herself out a side door into the yard. Through a gentle veil of snowflakes, she trekked across the lawn toward the trees to the north, nearer the river. At first, the strong brew comforted her, but eventually, she returned to her diatribe against Abby.

"Where is justice in this life? Why are babies born to women unfit to be mothers, while others long for them, but are denied the blessing. And don't tell me God cares."

Letting herself remember, Cal thought of her own mother, the perfect picture of maternal instinct and affection. She had adored her only daughter, spent most of her time with her, playing and teaching and loving. And when Cal's father returned from work, both of them devoted themselves to their child, albeit, with good boundaries for her to grow into. That's what parents should be like. Totally dedicated to their

41

children. Selflessly giving.

No doubt Abby was given free rein in her life, allowed anything and everything, spoiled and cooed over, but not properly raised. No moral boundaries. No direction. What kind of parent did that? Were they still out there somewhere, with no thought to their daughter? Did they know of their grandchild?

When Cal reached the trees, the snow had accumulated. She had to step high to keep going, but that was a simple physical challenge. As she pushed on, she felt a lightness of heart. Freedom in her aloneness. Peace in the stillness. Comfort in her physical abilities. But then her memory betrayed her into thinking about forbidden things. Yes, her childhood had been golden, her parents the best. But they failed by their final abdication—dying and leaving her alone in the world.

She raised her chin and let the December sunshine kiss her face. It was a good thing she had come to terms with their sudden abandonment. At least she thought she had. In this strange little town, she couldn't stop her brain or her emotions from working against her.

Cal abruptly did an about-face and headed back into the thickening snow. No more memories. She had remembered all she could, all there was. The rest was locked away. Absolutely no trespassing. Dragging in a deep breath, she thought again of Abby, and committed herself to make sure the baby was okay, that Abby's selfishness didn't jeopardize her child. Maybe that's why Cal had arrived here in Happenstance, to alleviate a tragic event. One could never be sure.

Bear always brought sunshine into Joel's day, no matter what was eating him. And there was a lot.

"Take a load off, fella." Bear offered Joel a Styrofoam cup of water. "Since you're not man enough for my brew."

"Yeah, right. Just looking to my survival. By the way, have you met Sandy yet?"

Bear poured himself a cup of sludge and eased into his torn vinyl chair, leaning back into it until Joel expected the whole thing to pop apart with the strain. "Oh, I've met Sandy. Way back when he was a humble dendrologist in Lakeview Forest. Crazy Irish leprechaun he was...still is. Except for the fact that he's lean and tall. Comes and goes on a whim."

"He must have had some good whims, since they resulted in a PhD."

Bear saluted Joel with his coffee cup. "You got that right. He's smart as a wick but doesn't flout it."

"You mean flaunt it?"

"Huh?"

Joel decided it wouldn't pay to correct Bear's verbal misnomers. "Nothing."

"Anyway," continued Bear, "he was here this mornin' at six."

"Six? You open the shop that early?"

"Not for customers. But I gotta have my shop coffee goin' in case somebody needs a visit!" He guffawed and took another lethal swig. "Me and Sandy had ourselves a good chinwag before the rest of the world woke up. Somethin' pure and sweet about the early mornin'."

"I agree, in most cases," said Joel. "Except for the sludge you serve."

"Hey, gimme a break. I do my best. By the way, you seen Sandy's protégé? I hear tell she's surprising." Bear's bushy brows rose.

"Yeah, she's interesting all right. She's at the hotel, but we see her mostly in passing. She's not much of a people person. What do you think makes a nice young woman wear all that metal and ink?"

"Maybe you hit your nail with a hammer there, Joel. Maybe there's a reason she expresses herself like that. I got no idea what that might be, but there's gotta be somethin'."

Joel thought about that. He had formed a fast judgment without knowing any of the facts. Not that he could know what had happened to Cal to make her like she was, but he should reconsider his preconceived ideas. He would ask Abby how she felt about Cal. She might be more discerning.

"What you got on your mind, kid, since I know you didn't come for the coffee."

"How perceptive of you."

"I ain't nothin' if not preceptive."

Joel tamped down his snort of laughter and reminded himself that this man had both wisdom and compassion, gathered through his years. Grammar and word usage didn't figure in. His ways were endearing, not annoying. "Worrying about Abby. She still wants to go find her aunt in Ainsworth, but I doubt she'll find her there."

"Why not?"

"The aunt hasn't answered any of Abby's calls. It's been years, and I mean like a decade, since Abby has seen her. She's elderly. No idea what could have happened between then and now."

"Hmm." Bear paused before answering. "First of all, kid, you ain't doin' yourself any favors by worryin'. No help there. Two, is there anything you can do about it? Seems to me you have to wait and be patient for now."

Joel nodded. "I know. Dr. Paula suggested I talk to Constable Rising Moon, since she's pretty good at finding people. I did contact her. Now I have to wait, but sometimes it helps to talk it through, you know?"

A wide smile warmed Bear's face. "Then you come to the right place. Any time you got yourself a conundrum, you got a chair here, and a listening ear."

Conundrum. Huh. He got that one right. Go figure. "You haven't seen the last of me," said Joel. "Thanks for listening...again. Have a good one."

"You too, kid. Keep your chins up."

Chapter 6

Joel received the constable's return call that evening while they were having dinner. He excused himself and answered.

"Constable Rising Moon?"

"Hey, Joel. Sorry to interrupt your dinner. It's pretty fine fare, as I hear."

"It is," he said, his fingers tapping on the end table in the parlor.

"I found out some things," she said, all business. "Do you mind if I drop by the hotel to talk with both you and Abby?"

"No problem."

"Okay. I'm at the end of the lane. Be there in a jiffy."

Joel returned to the dining room and sent Abby a wink, then tilted his head in the direction of the hallway. Puzzled, she excused herself and joined him. Joel took her elbow and led her farther from the door. "Constable Rising Moon called. She found out something about your aunt, and she's dropping by shortly to talk with us."

"What—?"

"She didn't tell me. We'll have to—"

The doorbell rang and the constable stepped inside, nodding at them. "Is there someplace we can talk?"

Matt, on his way to answer the door, said, "Come behind the counter into the Barlows' office. It'll give you privacy." He led them through, then left and closed the door behind him.

Abby nodded at Constable Rising Moon. "Constable. What's the news?"

"Call me Priscilla, and please take a seat."

Abby, Joel and Priscilla claimed comfy armchairs.

"I've found some news about your aunt, Abby. The house in Ainsworth, listed as the property of a Miss Evelyn Turner, has been empty more than two years."

"Two years! Why wouldn't she let me know she was moving?"

Joel raised an eyebrow. "How could she, when she had no idea where you were?"

"As far as I can discover," continued Priscilla, "there are

no children or next of kin on record."

"That's because she doesn't have any children."

"And how exactly are you related to her?"

Abby sent a swift glance toward Joel, then faced the constable again. "She is my aunt, my mother's sister."

Priscilla pressed her lips together and typed a note into her phone. "I don't have any record of your mother either."

Joel, sensing Abby's frustration, filled in the gap, telling Priscilla about the lifestyle of Abby's folks, and their avoidance of connections.

"I see," said the officer. "What puzzles me is the disparity in ages. You look to be about twenty, so your mother could be forty or fifty. But Evelyn Turner is 83, according to the records."

"That can't be right." Abby fidgeted in her seat.

Joel stepped in again. "Do you think maybe she was your mother's aunt, Abby? Not her sister?"

"Well, I..." she turned to stare at him, as if searching for answers on his face. "I suppose she could have been. I called her 'aunt,' so I assumed. Never worried about actual ages." She turned back to Priscilla. "But do you know where she is? Is she dead?"

"No," said the constable. "She seems to have taken up residence—or perhaps I should say she's been moved—to a nursing home for seniors in Florida."

"Florida! Then we have to go there, Joel. We have to find her. I'd still like to stay with her, or at least nearby. Besides my parents, who don't give a care, she's the only family I remember that's ever taken an interest in me."

Her automatic use of the word "we" startled Joel. One day she claimed she didn't need him, the next that she expected him to be there.

"I'd stall that visit if I were you." Priscilla glanced at Joel. "Go on."

"She was apparently suffering from dementia long before she was moved to Florida."

"Dementia? Nursing home? How did she end up in Florida, anyway?" Abby reached for Joel's hand, and he warmed at the fact that she was actually seeking his support.

"The receptionist at the home said Eve had written a

letter years ago that she wished to end her days at *The Aging Sages Rest Home,* should she ever need to leave her house. When Eve didn't answer their annual calls, they made arrangements to have her moved. I'm sure there's a will, but I have yet to locate it or the contents thereof.

"That's all I have. I'd advise you to hire a lawyer and find out if she has a living will or something of that sort. Set up the fact that you are next of kin, or contact your mother, and let the authorities sort it out as soon as possible."

Abby stood and reached out a hand to Constable Rising Moon. "Thank you for bringing me the news. I appreciate your research."

"I enjoy research, just sorry it was not the news you were expecting or hoping for."

"That's not your problem. You accomplished more than I ever could."

Joel thanked the constable, planning to see her to the door, but as soon as they exited the tiny office, Miss Emmaline's voice called out. "Priscilla, dear, do come and say hello to everyone."

Priscilla smiled as she shook her head. She poked her head into the parlor, where everyone had moved in the interim, and greeted them. Joel watched her, seeing again the close-knit community where they all seemed to know one another.

However, the officer's gaze lingered a moment on Cal as she scanned the room. Cal sat farther from the group. When she noticed a uniformed policewoman watching her, she turned to pick up the magazine she had dropped to the floor and hid her face in it. Strange reaction. Why did a police presence affect her that way? Was Joel misinterpreting Priscilla's interest or Cal's fear of being discovered? He didn't think so, but he did wonder what had caught the officer's attention. Apparently, he wasn't the only one who wondered about Cal. The woman seemed to relax a bit once Priscilla left.

Abby tried to sidestep the parlor to go check on Noelle, but Emmaline called her inside.

"Noelle is fine," she said. "Graycie and I took a peek and

your little monitor hasn't made a sound. Come sit with us. We're talking about Christmas."

"It will take your mind off your Aunt Eve," whispered Joel.

Abby noticed Cal's eyes dart from her to Joel, then she resumed reading her magazine, without turning the pages.

"This living nativity," resumed Emmaline, "is a most fascinating endeavor. I think it will bring to life the story of Jesus. And certainly, it will be a challenge getting the whole town involved."

Abby tried to let the present claim her attention. The idea of an entire town portraying the story of the nativity perplexed Abby, as she'd only ever thought of Christmas as lights and color and gifts. And Santa, of course. These people were talking about something entirely different—that Christmas was Jesus' birthday. She'd seen the baby in the manger in stores and displays, but had never given it a thought beyond that.

"Why do you celebrate the birth of a baby for so many years? It's just a story."

All eyes turned to Abby, or, to be clear, turned on her.

"My dear Abigail." Emmaline reached over and placed her hand over Abby's. "Jesus isn't just a baby born in a stable. He grew up, you know, was hated by religious leaders who felt he was a threat. They killed him because of that."

"Killed him?" Now Abby was more confused. "What did he do to make them so angry?"

"He said he was God's Son." Joel took up the story, and Abby couldn't believe he'd known all this and she'd never heard it.

"Well then," said Abby, "he asked for their disgust. That's a declaration and a half."

Emmaline squeezed her hand. "But he is God's Son, my dear. We couldn't meet God's demands, his holiness. Because God loves us, he sent Jesus to die in our place."

"Whoa." She thought about that. "You mean he saved us?"

"Exactly," said Matt. "That's why we remember Christmas. He did it all for love."

The room became quiet, everyone deep in thought until

Cal spoke up, her face hard, her words tainted by anger. "And now we can all live happily ever after." She rose abruptly, threw the magazine onto her chair and stalked from the room. After half a minute, they heard the door of the chapel slam. Abby felt Cal's anger lingering in the room.

Shocked silence fell until Sandy spoke. "Forgive her, if you please. From the little I've gathered, she's had some hard knocks in her life, but I'll not be knowing the details."

Before anyone else could respond, they heard voices at the entrance of the hotel as a group of carolers sang out together: *Away in a manger, no crib for a bed...*

"I love carolers," said Emmaline, standing to move to the door. "Perhaps Johanna would..."

Before she could finish her thoughts, Johanna appeared in the doorway and handed Matt a plate of delectable cookies and a bowl of Christmas oranges to share with the singers. Matt did the honors, and spoke with the group for a few minutes, some of them students of his. They then sang *Joy to the World*, and *We Wish You a Merry Christmas*, after which they repeated their thanks for the treats, trooped outside and piled into vehicles to move on to the next place on their list.

When the other guests left the parlor, Joel took a seat beside Abby. After listening to the singing, he asked her, "How are you doing?"

She dropped her head onto the back of the sofa and closed her eyes. "I don't know. First, my plans have been changed beyond salvaging, and second, I have no other plans."

"As true as that is, the authorities will want to talk to your mother, since she is closer to Eve than you are. At least in chronology."

"You know my parents. They won't even know. Or care."

"They'd care, Abby. I'm sure they would. Eve was close with your mother, from what you've told me. I even let my parents know where I am, and we're not at all close."

"I guess you don't know my folks as well as you think. They are confirmed free spirits, no ties, no holds, no worries of any kind to hold them back from living freely."

"But, Abby, surely they'll want to know they have a grandchild."

"They won't care." Abby couldn't keep her tears from

escaping down her cheeks. "What am I going to do now, Joel?"

Just as they were contemplating the situation, Cal entered the room. When she saw them, she pulled up short, then, without another word, left the hotel. She didn't snarl, but Abby could hear it anyway.

"What is up with that woman?" asked Abby. "Looks like she's afraid of something. She's so angry."

Joel shrugged. "I have no idea, and no way to find out. Besides, right now, we have our own web to untangle."

Again, the word "we." Abby squeezed his hand, brushed her tears away and pushed herself to her feet. "I need to get some sleep before Noelle wakes up. Thanks for listening."

Cal pulled her scarf more tightly around her neck. It was colder outside than she'd anticipated, but Sandy would be waiting for her. She had no idea why he wanted her to come out to the forest after dark, but she'd learned to trust the Irishman. He was a good soul, even though he had his quirks.

She was late because she had given in to self-pity. Again. And that unexpected burst of anger. Something about this town had her on edge. She wanted to hide, to avoid everyone and everything, but all her emotions raged inside, robbing her hard-won self-control.

Marching along Main Street North, under the light of the streetlamps, she soon came to the entrance to Lakeview Forest. Now, where was Sandy? He was like a ghost some days.

"Sandy? Where are you hiding?"

She trudged on through the forest, using her flashlight, stepping high in the snow, her eyes sharp as she stared around her.

"Beautiful, in'it?"

Cal jumped and turned in one motion, almost falling over a dead tree limb. She steadied herself. "How do you do that?"

"What's that?"

"You know very well. You appear out of nowhere, like you were a forest spirit."

Sandy's pale eyebrows rose and fell a few times, then he laughed. "Please aim that light away from me face. All righty.

On with the work. Tell me, minion, what do trees do in winter? What have I taught you?"

At his normal conversation, Cal relaxed. That's all she wanted. A sense of normalcy and something physical to do. Something to think about other than memories. "They're dormant. Their life processes slow to conserve energy so they can get through the winter. They produce very little, if any, oxygen in winter."

"Very well done, Miss—"

"Cal. Just Cal. You know that, Sandy."

Sandy huffed. "Well, Cal of the Blazing Eyes, what do you plan to do in winter, these long, dark evenings at the hotel? Play bridge or canasta with the Barlow sisters? Talk of today's failing education system with Matthew? Or maybe you'd prefer speaking of baby things with that Abby girl—"

"Leave it alone, Sandy."

"Can't avoid what I don't know about, now can I? You'd do well to open up to somebody, even if that not be me." He gave her a moment, then said, "Set your troubles aside for a time, love. I have something to show you."

"What?" She could not disengage from her anger so easily, but she wanted to see what he was referring to. He was always full of surprises. She'd take anything that distracted her from the reality of her past.

"Come and see." He moved back through a stand of ponderosa pines and into a hidden clearing. "Wait here."

She stood still while Sandy crouched behind a large evergreen, then she gasped in delight. The whole clearing sparkled with tiny fairy lights, like a sky full of stars, only in the trees. Under the sheltering arms of the large fir sat a crudely made cradle. It was empty, but Cal knew it was meant for the Baby Jesus. Gathered around were figures of shepherds and...on second look, she realized they were rough garments draped over smaller trees and shrubs. A couple of bushes were garlanded with white cloth, resembling sheep. Ingenious. So that's what he'd been spending his time on lately.

"Sandy, this is amazing." Words failed her for a time as she tried to take it all in. Then reality slipped in. "Are you going to invite others to see this?" She hoped they were not on the way here already, or she'd duck out right now.

"No, ma'am. This be for you and me. Just a special secret garden to contemplate the miracle."

"But how did you get electricity all the way out here?"

Sandy was as elusive with his answer as he was about appearing out of nowhere. "No need for you to worry about that, now. Part of the miracle."

Cal shook her head in wonder. She sat on a conveniently placed tree stump, and knew all at once that she was alone. The Irish sprite had disappeared, leaving her to delight in the beauty of light and peace, with no company but the faithful trees. She took a deep breath of the sharp clear air, leaned her head into her hands, and wept.

Chapter 7

"I'll stay as long as she needs me." Joel pretended to take a sip of Bear's coffee as he sat across the littered office deck from the big man. He could not drink it, or the rest of his day would be plagued by heartburn and upset stomach. "She's lost. I can't leave her now."

Bear gulped down the rest of his "used oil" and tossed the cup into the overfull trash can, where it rolled onto the floor to join others of its ilk beneath his desk. "Hmm."

He caught Joel's eyes, and the younger man tensed, sure Bear would give him a lecture on letting go, on not enabling the young woman. He'd heard it all before, mostly in his own mind, argument after argument surrounding Abby's situation and what his response should be. He didn't need more options, he needed guidance. That's why he'd created an excuse to help Bear at his shop this morning. The indecision was eating at him.

"You got to ask yourself some basic questions, Joel, like what does Abby need? What can you do to help? How much of your time are you willin' to give up for her? What's your motivation?"

"I've asked myself all those questions repeatedly," growled Joel. "I don't know the best thing for her. I didn't think I was enabling her. I don't know why I've stayed this long or come this far...No, wait. I know that. I already told you."

"Yeah. You love her." Bear whistled a non-descript tune between his teeth and leaned back, his vinyl chair squealing in protest. He looked up at the ceiling and closed his eyes.

"The answer isn't up there," said Joel. "I've looked. Not in the ceiling, not in the stars, not even on the back of my eyelids."

"I ain't lookin' for your answers in my fallin' down ceilin'. I'm sayin' a prayer for wisdom, cuz God knows you need it. You'd do well to do the same."

Joel felt ashamed by his lack of response. He'd been raised in the home of a preacher, but that didn't mean it was a good place. More guilt than glory, from his experience. But he hadn't thrown away his beliefs altogether.

Bear interrupted his thoughts. "Did Abby ask you to help her?"

"No."

"Does she expect you to stay indefinitely, as her protector?"

"Protector? No. She wanted to go alone."

"Why did you stick with her, besides the fact of love?"

Joel's frustration mounted again. "I told you, she's lost. She has never met circumstances before that she couldn't handle, and now she's responsible for two lives. It's starting to hit her."

"Her parents won't help?"

"Nope. They did their bit until she was eighteen, at least gave her a roof over her head and food to eat. She's on her own. But yesterday she asked me what she should do. She's never asked anyone for help before. Well, except when she was giving birth."

Bear hissed. "Breaks my heart. Now, answer me this: if I told you exactly what to do right now, would you do it?"

The corner of Joel's mouth tipped in a smile. "Depends if it made any sense."

"To who?"

"To me."

"And if you agreed it was wise, and you told Abby to do it, would she follow through?"

This time Joel laughed. "Never. You don't tell Abby to do anything. She makes up her own mind."

"But you told me she as much as asked you what she should do."

"Yeah," said Joel, "but she rarely follows my suggestions. And we're not married or anything, so why should she? You ever married, Bear?"

"Me? Nope. Never had the opportunity. But I am a good observer."

"Better go." Joel pushed his chair back and wedged his full cup into the side of the trash can. "This isn't getting me anywhere."

"What were you expectin'? I ain't no GSP. I can't give you

directions through to the end of your dilemma. All I can do is tell you one piece of wisdom my daddy told me: when you don't know what to do next, do the next thing."

"What?"

"Just think about it. What should you do right now?"

"Go get some decent coffee from Sol at the Bistro."

Bear laughed so hard Joel was sure the old office chair would pop its final screws.

"You got it! Go do it, and then the next step will show up. It's like drivin' in the dark, kid. You can only go as far as the light guides you." Bear wiped his eyes with the back of his hand.

After a satisfying latte with a cream leaf design on top, Joel trudged back to the hotel. The air was cool but refreshing, and he needed to clear his head. As he took these next steps, he mulled over what he would say to Abby. She needed to get a handle on reality, responsibility, on the fact that the life of little Noelle depended directly on her. How would he open that conversation without offending her?

When he stepped inside the hotel, the cheery sunroom warmed him, the long hallway welcomed him in a way no other place had in a very long time. He almost wished he hadn't stopped by Sol's bistro, because Johanna might now have a treat just as tasty. As he passed by the dining room, he saw a note on the table beside a tall glass of water with ice cubes and a floating slice of lemon. The note said: *Enough coffee you have this day.* Joel chuckled, and guzzled the cool, flavored water.

Now, where was Abby? He should talk to her about an alternate plan to going to Ainsworth. He hoped she didn't send him packing as soon as he voiced his concerns.

At that moment, Abby poked her head out of her bedroom and called to him. "Joel, where have you been? I've been waiting to talk to you."

He advanced toward her, then peeked into the room to see little Noelle lying awake in her bed, while on her own bed, Abby was arranging a wide variety of articles.

"What are you doing?"

She laughed. "What does it look like? I'm preparing to raise my daughter. The Barlow sisters asked Maisie from the hair salon to stop at the thrift store in Athens for some little outfits for Noelle, and they also asked her to bring several packages of disposable diapers. Maisie also brought some of the baby things she kept since her youngest was born. She said she was happy to get them out of her storage space, especially for someone who needs them. Isn't this great? These people are truly kind."

"I'll say," replied Joel, when he could find his voice. "Over and above."

"Yes, and Dr. Paula is stopping by later today to check up on both of us. I don't see the need, since we're both doing well, but she insisted, so I let her come. She's more than a doctor; she's becoming a friend. Who knew?"

Joel pondered all this and wondered how strong Bear's prayers were. Things seemed to be falling into place for Abby and Noelle. Except, of course, a place to live and a way to earn a living. He'd better get with the praying too, if he really cared about her. He had some catching up to do with God.

As Abby sorted through the pile of clothing Maisie Macdonald had brought, she marveled at what some people gave away. This stuff was good quality and pretty, too. She'd had no idea how it would feel to have a daughter. Her little princess.

Sometimes she was afraid this unexpected maternal instinct would desert her and she wouldn't know how to mother her child. She wondered if her mother had felt this way about her, and if so, where had that feeling gone? She'd always been looked after, part of the family, of the home, but had her mother ever felt this overwhelming passion to protect her little girl? She tried to convince herself that her mom didn't have a strong maternal instinct, but if she were honest with herself, she'd have to admit Mom was self-absorbed. She needed to be free to express herself without too much distraction from others.

That's how I've been all my life. Selfish. Concerned only with how things work out for me. I can't do that anymore.

She hadn't been brave enough to discuss with Joel the things she'd been thinking. After all, she didn't need to burden him with her affairs. Although, he seemed interested. Her thoughts headed along that tangent until she stopped them and brought them back on track. Enough about Joel. She had to work this out herself.

As Christmas quickly approached, Abby decided it would be best if she and Noelle stayed at the hotel until after the holidays. She had already asked the ladies if this was an option, to which they said they would not allow her to leave until she was ready. Those two were something else.

Once Christmas was past, she'd begin sending out feelers for jobs, and possibly a place to stay nearby. And she wouldn't have to live in the same establishment as Cal. Maybe that woman and Sandy would move on then, too. This was apparently just a stop-off for them. She could always hope.

Abby didn't want to leave this town where people seemed to have her back, and were in love with Noelle. Maybe she could have coffee with Maisie and ask her some questions. Even with their difference in age, Maisie felt like a friend who, for some reason, seemed to understand and accept her.

Abby pulled out her cellphone and hit Maisie's number. They had exchanged contact info when Maisie delivered the used clothing. They arranged to meet for coffee at Happenstance Bistro & Books the next morning, and Abby could hardly wait. She had this hope of a new life dancing just beyond her grasp, and she didn't want to lose sight of it.

Next day, mid-morning, Abby lifted little Noelle from her crib and carried her outside, where she set her into the stroller Maisie had lent her. She tucked the warm blankets snugly around her and set out with a light step, pushing the buggy along the lane. The air was crisp and fresh, but not too cold, and the sunshine warmed her soul.

She knew Joel would have jumped to help her, but she had not told him she was going, and he had disappeared as well, maybe to Bear's. He went there often. Anyway, this was not a long walk, only the length of the lane, then across the town square—town oval, Abby corrected herself—and into

Happenstance Bistro & Books.

As it was ten in the morning, the coffee crowd had gathered, and the hum of voices and laughter filled the big old building with a unique ambiance against the backdrop of an eclectic assortment of music. A happy place. Checking around her, Abby spotted Maisie, who rose to take the stroller to her table.

"Order whatever you want, Abby. It's on me."

"I think not," said the barista. "I haven't seen you here before, so it's on us. Yours too, Maisie, since you invited your friend."

"Thanks, Sol. You're the best."

An elderly man who had invaded the barista's space mumbled, "That's what you think. I've seen the real Sol, and believe me, he's far from the best."

Abby stared at him, but Sol said, "Don't listen to Morris. He's an old grouch."

Morris glared at them both in turn. "At least I'm honest. And I do believe you have stooped to ageism, Solomon. I shall have to report this."

"Go ahead, chum. See who listens."

Maisie came up behind her and whispered, "Don't pay any attention to them. They think they're standup comedians, but they're rarely as funny as they think."

Abby quirked her eyebrows and took a deep breath. "I'll have a tall vanilla bean latte, hot, or whatever you would call that on your menu, and one of those lemon tarts, please. Are they Johanna's?"

"You bet, ma'am. She is a baker supreme."

"Yes, I know. I've been staying at the hotel, and her food is super."

"I'm Sol, by the way. Owner and operator of this fine establishment." He glanced over his shoulder.

"Yes, I heard your self-praise," answered Morris, on his way to the back, past the sign that indicated a lending library.

Sol snickered. "Don't let Morris bother you. It's his only form of entertainment, putting people down. Me in particular."

"I had more positive entertainment walking here from the hotel," Abby laughed. "My name is Abby Maguire, and the little princess in the stroller is my daughter, Noelle." She stuck out her hand and they shook.

"Nice to meet you, Abby. Is it Abigail?"

"Yes, why do you ask?"

"My mother's name. She is the real deal. The epitome of charming."

Abby smiled. "I'd love to meet her. Not sure how long I'll be here, but people are amazingly friendly and helpful."

"This place is very accepting," he said, "and I don't think there's anyone here who hasn't been shown the friendliness of the townspeople. A remarkable place. You might want to stay a while."

She laughed. "You sound like Bear."

At his crestfallen expression, she corrected herself. "No, I mean that sounds like what he would say."

"Phew. Thanks for that. Here you go, Abby." He passed her the latte and lemon tart. "Enjoy. I'll bring Maisie's order to the table."

"I was all excited about meeting this little angel," said Maisie, "but it seems the buggy ride has put her to sleep."

"She's a great sleeper." Abby set her food on the table and took a seat. "But she's also getting more vocal when she's awake. Lots to get used to. I don't know what I'd do without the Barlow sisters." She glanced over at Maisie. "They're old, and neither has kids that I'm aware of, yet they seem to know how to help me."

Maisie's smile widened. "Let me tell you why."

Abby settled in to sip and munch and listen, while Maisie told her a bit about her past.

"I came here alone, unwell and pregnant, and they took me in. No questions, no judgment, only love and caring. I can't tell you how much they did for me."

Abby stared. "You're kidding. You were just where I am now. What happened?"

"Oh, a fair bit. They gave me a place to stay, and the former hairdresser hired me and trained me on the job, while the ladies and others in the community looked after Zachary."

"Did your parents approve?"

"My parents didn't know. I had distanced myself from them, and the father of my baby didn't know I was pregnant."

"Oh wow. Did you ever tell him?"

"Much later. In fact, not that long ago. Turned out, his mother had kept that information from him, although she knew it, and it caused quite a kerfuffle when it finally became known. But he is now married to a lovely girl, and they have a nice relationship with Zach. And I am married to a most wonderful man. We share two more kids."

"Happy endings." Abby sipped her delicious latte. "I wish I believed in them, but I think you have to create your own ending."

Little Noelle shifted in her buggy but fell back to sleep.

"When I was young," said Maisie, "those create-your-own-ending books were all the rage. You could skip from one scenario to the next one you chose, and so on until you had found a suitable route to an ending of your choice. I think that's kind of like life. There are many options, many possibilities that may occur, depending on your decisions along the way. If you don't mind, I'll be praying that you choose the right paths on your journey."

Abby thought about what Maisie had said. "You can pray if you want, but I don't much believe in God. Joel does." She glanced up at Maisie, wishing she could take back that last comment. It didn't matter what Joel believed.

Maisie reached across the table and rested her hand on Abby's. "Don't worry. Let the things in your heart find their way out. Happenstance tends to encourage that somehow. And you don't have to believe, but I do. In fact, our reverend, Otto Selig, is very approachable, and may be able to offer you some assistance while you're here."

"I've met him and his wife. Another case of them being too old to understand me. I don't mean to offend; I'm just being honest."

"You can be honest with me, but don't underestimate the Seligs. They have had many experiences that have shaped them into the caring people they are. And I'm thinking you and Noelle might enjoy their spare room if you're interested. They have no children—well, they did have one, but she passed away at a very young age—and they absolutely love helping people."

"I keep learning unexpected things about folks from this

town." Abby finished her pastry and sipped the last of her beverage. "I am becoming very judgmental, and it surprises me. I've never been that way, or at least I didn't realize I was. I must try to keep an open mind. I've never had much to do with elderly people."

"We'll all be there eventually, Lord willing," said Maisie. "They have a lot to offer."

The women chatted about lighter things and parted much later, in time for Abby to stroll back to the hotel for one of Johanna's simple yet delicious lunches. Today it was minestrone soup and chicken salad sandwiches. What a morning it had been, all this unexpected information, all the new people, the vibrant sense of life she felt here in Happenstance. Maybe she should stay a while. "Might do me good." She laughed at herself for quoting Bear. Could be he was a lot smarter than one thought at first glance.

She wanted to tell Joel all about her morning, and only managed to hold in her eagerness when she thought about how he might receive her sharing of her thoughts. She'd take her time.

Cal scratched at her head; the wool cap irritated her scalp. When Sandy had dropped her off at the bistro, she'd had opportunity to watch Abby and the other woman from the farthest corner of the place. Maisie or something. They seemed to enjoy their visit, although she didn't know when Abby had a chance to get to know people here. It hadn't been a week, if she figured correctly.

Just as she lifted her empty cup for another swallow, the proprietor showed up. "I can get you another cappuccino, ma'am, or a regular coffee. No charge either way, since it's your first visit here."

"Thanks," she said, surprised by his kindness. "I'll have coffee if that's what you have with you."

"Good choice," he said. "My regular coffee is extremely good."

A gruff voice caught Cal's attention from across the divider between bistro and library. "That's quite the self-praise—again," it said.

Sol laughed. "This is Morris, our resident grouch. Morris, meet...ah..."

"Cal."

"Meet Cal. And please, Cal, don't let him get you down."

When Sol had left to refill other cups, Morris said, "Doesn't look like you need any more discouragement. I'll leave you be."

What did he mean? Did she look that bad? Maybe it was the hat, but she hadn't wanted Abby to recognize her. The shade of her hair immediately gave her away. But she couldn't cover the eyebrow and nose rings. *Nobody's concern but mine.*

Was Morris right? Did she carry her burden that noticeably? She thought she'd hidden it well, but then, she couldn't watch herself. Whatever, it seemed impossible to avoid contact with people around here. Who knew this out-of-the-way hamlet would be the friendliest place in Nebraska?

She swallowed the rest of the warm coffee, then headed out of the bistro to make sure Abby managed to get the baby home safely. Couldn't trust that girl. Anyone knew it was too cold to take a tiny baby outside in this northern weather.

When Joel showed up in the dining room at lunchtime, he was pleased to see Abby and Noelle there. The little princess lay squirming in a car seat carrier, while the ladies sat across from them.

"Matthew is busy with details for the living nativity, so he said he'd grab a bite at the Seligs'." Emmaline tasted her soup. "Mmm. Johanna's soup calms the very soul. It's the best."

"I agree it's very tasty," said Grayce, "but we cannot know it is the best, because we have not sampled all other soups by all other chefs."

"Oh bother, Graycie. Why do you try to irritate me? I am simply enjoying our repast and expressing my gratitude for its quality. Do try to be more positive."

"Honesty and realism are always best, sister dear."

Shaking her head, Emmaline turned to Joel. "Do tell us what you've learned about the progress of the nativity project. I look forward to experiencing it in person in a few days."

"It involves a lot of work on the part of many of the people around town," said Joel. "I tagged along with Matt for a while, and I can't believe how much time and effort he and the reverend and many others are putting into it. Even Mayor Wuppertal, and he's Jewish."

"Anything for the town," said Emmaline.

"The nativity will be set up in Mr. Alkmaar's dairy barn, just west along Main Street North." Joel drained his soup bowl. The contents tasted great, and he wasn't even a lover of soup. "There will be an angel choir set up in the fields between Jerry Alkmaar's land and the town, and he plans to move some of his sheep there. The shepherds will look after them."

"I hope they don't take off when the angels sing." Abby's face had begun to sparkle at Joel's descriptions. "I was reading that part in Miss Grayce's Bible, and it sounds like material for an exciting community pageant. If the weather holds up, I can bring Noelle out to watch it."

"Sure. I'll take you two on the grand tour. The committee is planning to bring in horse-drawn wagons to move people from one station to the next. Main Street all around the square will feature various bazaars and shops."

Joel's heart warmed at the happiness he saw in Abby's face, and the look of love she gave to Noelle when she picked up the squirming baby almost made his heart stop. What could he do with all this emotion? It was more, much more, than he had expected. Maybe the change in Abby had caused it.

Emmaline's voice broke his reverie. "Do Graycie and I have a part to play?"

"Actually, you do. Happenstance Hotel is the Bethlehem Inn."

"I can't say I approve of that involvement." Emmaline's face fell. "I don't want to turn away Mary and Joseph."

"It's only a play," commented Abby. "We need everyone."

Her use of the word "we" gave Joel a shock. Was she planning to stay? Had she made some kind of plan? Had Happenstance pulled her into its welcoming warmth? But what was he supposed to do? Forget his dream of becoming a doctor? Stay here in Happenstance and help Abby? Or leave and deal with a broken heart? He could use a hint.

Chapter 8

Since Joel had been helping him when he could, Bear had caught up on his jobs at the shop and decided to stop by the hotel to see how two of his favorite customers were doing.

He rang the bell and stepped inside the sunny entry. They called this a solarium, he remembered. A place for the sun to shine in through the long windows. "Hello the house," he called, as he tromped along the hallway.

"Come join us in the parlor."

The thin voice of Miss Grayce made him smile, although the sound also gave him pause. She was getting fragile, this dear woman. Good thing she had Miss Emmaline to keep her feisty. Those two were a good team. Entertaining too.

He entered the parlor, but stopped when he saw the other guest. As he'd heard, the woman was a sight to behold. Like a neon light. Ink all over, more earrings than a jewelry store. And that hair. Looked to him like she was tryin' to scare away the bogeyman. With all the grace he could muster, he welcomed her. "Hey there, ma'am. I'm Gavin Beresford, otherwise known as Bear. Haven't seen you around these parts before."

She nodded. "That's because I haven't been here before. Name's Cal."

"Do sit down, Bear," said Grayce. "You are too big to stand. We can't see around you."

"Yes, ma'am." He took a chair farthest from Cal and relaxed as Johanna brought him a cup of steaming coffee. She set a plate of muffins on the table and left.

"Time off, Mr. Beresford?" Emmaline shifted to face him and waited for his answer.

"Appears so, ma'am. With Joel helpin' me, I'm all caught up. Unless somebody drives another weary vehicle onto my lot."

"That's nice, especially at Christmas time," Emmaline continued. "Do you have a part in the nativity presentation?"

"I sure do. I happen to be the farrier. I may not know much about horses, but I got the muscle to hold up their feet and pretend to trim their hooves."

"Takes more than muscle to be a farrier." Cal stared at him, seeming to invite an argument.

"I'm sure you're right, ma'am, but—"

"Stop calling me ma'am. Just Cal will do."

He swallowed his first response. "Well now, I will try to do that, Cal. Forgive me if I forget, as my mama taught me to be respectful of women."

"My name is not disrespectful."

Bear nodded and turned away from her. "Supposed to be a mild Christmas." He knew it sounded silly but he said the first thing that came to his mind.

Grayce responded. "Yes. That will be a very good thing for the nativity."

Emmaline chose to differ. "And when have the weather forecasters ever been correct? They suggest a few days of the expected, then throw in anything that pleases. And that changes in a day or two. I watch it on my weather app."

"Weather app!" Grayce's voice dripped with sarcasm. "Indeed."

Bear pushed away irritation with Cal. "You got that right, Miss Emmaline, but I do hope they're right this time. Ain't no fun pretendin' to trim horse hooves on a cold winter day."

A few minutes later, Abby joined them, little Noelle sleeping in her arms. She settled near Cal, who rose and left the room. They watched her go, wordless.

"I think she dislikes babies," whispered Abby. "She refuses to be in the same room with Noelle."

"Must be a reason," said Bear, trying to be fair to Cal in spite of his allowing his first impressions to rule.

"Whatever it is, it's not Noelle's fault."

"I know, Abby. Ain't nobody's fault, but there's somethin' eatin' that woman."

———————

At dinner that evening, a long envelope lay beside Joel's place at the table. One glance and he knew where it came from. He slipped the envelope into the back pocket of his jeans and hoped no one had seen. He glanced at Abby; her eyes were fastened on his, questions shooting silently at him. She could be perceptive for someone who usually concentrated on herself.

Again, in contrast with her usual outspokenness, she did not say a word, but turned her attention to the gnocchi and fettuccini in cream sauce, garnished with fresh parsley grown in Johanna's winter window pots.

Joel found it difficult to eat. The food wanted to stick in his throat, tasty as it was, as if it would stop the words from coming out. The helpless "what now?" He had no doubt Abby would draw him aside after the meal and demand to know what was going on. And she did.

"Spill." Abby pulled him to the tiny library seat at the end of the long hallway beside the conservatory-cum-bedroom. She sat and patted the place next to her. "I can see it's bad news and you didn't even open the envelope."

"I can't tell you what it says. Would it be permissible for me to read my own mail first?"

"Joel. You have helped me more than I had even considered until lately, and now it's my turn. What's up?"

"It's a letter from the medical college I applied to way back when. That's all I know."

Abby was quiet for a bit, then solved his problem succinctly. "If you are rejected, nothing changes. If you're accepted, you pack your bags and hop a plane to college. What's difficult about that?"

Her directness made him sputter. "What's difficult? Don't you know?"

"Tell me."

Blowing out a big breath, Joel laid it on the line. "I don't want to leave you alone with Noelle. Raising a child is a huge responsibility. And I...I would find it very hard to leave her. I know she's nothing to me technically, but...there's this uncanny attachment. And not only with her."

Her eyes downcast, Abby stared at her hands, wringing them in her lap. Finally, she whispered her thoughts. "That's what I was afraid would happen. You shouldn't have come in the first place. I didn't ask you to. Now Noelle and I have become an obstacle to your dreams." She reached over and grabbed his hand. "I'm sorry this happened." She raised her eyes to his. "You have to leave and not look back. Forget about

SECRETS & SECOND CHANCES

us. We're not alone. There are a lot of caring people here, and I think I'll hang around for a while. At least, as long as the ladies let me stay here, or I find another place to stay, and until I get a job and a babysitter."

At the sound of Noelle's demanding cry next door, Abby stood, smiled sadly at him and floated from his presence. His chest hurt. He had to think. He pulled on his jacket and headed out into the winter day that had just dimmed to bleakness.

———————————

Abby blew her nose and checked her face in the mirror over the bureau. She took a long drink from her water bottle and picked up a clean and dry Noelle. She could not let Joel know how she felt. He had the right to his dreams, not to be dragged down by her situation. No, she had not invited him to come with her, but she honestly didn't know if she would have survived without him. He had helped her drive from Texas, bought some snacks along the way, stood by her side when Noelle was born, helped Bear fix her car, offered understanding and encouragement for the future. She felt bereft at the thought of his leaving, even though exhilarated at his acceptance into medical school. He would make a fantastic doctor.

Noelle, now calm and quiet, nestled into Abby's shoulder as they moved toward the voices coming from the parlor. Sounded like the Misses Barlow. Yes, that was Grayce speaking.

"We've turned away several groups now, Emm, because we didn't want our guests bothered by the crying of a baby. Not that the little angel is noisy. Not at all. But we must also consider how to support ourselves without the extra rooms under renovation."

"I can't believe what I'm hearing, Graycie. Since when did we ever turn someone away who needed our help? I simply cannot do it."

Abby stopped still, then returned the way she'd come. She arranged herself cross-legged on her bed, with Noelle cuddled in her arms. As she rocked her baby, she spoke soothingly to her. She jumped when a light knock sounded and Johanna entered, carrying a superbly created latte on a bed tray. All Abby could do was offer a weak thank you, and Johanna was gone before she could think of anything else to say. That strange woman always seemed to intuit when a snack or a hot drink was needed for comfort.

Abby settled Noelle on her lap and leaned over to sip the delicious drink. In between sips, she spoke her thoughts out loud, both her questions and her ideas, trying to arrange her jumbled thoughts. She had told Joel she'd be fine without him. But she'd been coddled. What would she do on her own? No one to spell her off. No one providing support and carrying the diaper garbage out to the bin. No one to cook meals for her. No ability to pay her way.

She finished the latte, complete with licking the sides of the cup, and set it aside as she tried to disengage herself from the emotions tearing at her. As the truth became real in her somehow altered reality, she broke into sobs. Noelle fixed her gaze on Abby. Who said babies were unaware? One moment Abby's world was as whole as it had ever been, and then everything began to fall apart, her heart included. And Noelle saw it all. Abby could no longer deny her feelings for Joel, although they might not be as strong as his for her. But in this town, the denial didn't make sense. Recognized or not, her feelings would push their way out.

Her crying jag subsided, and she held Noelle against her shoulder. She began telling her tiny daughter all about her woes, then stopped suddenly. No! She would not burden her daughter with her problems. The little angel didn't deserve that. Abby cleared her throat and began to quietly sing a lullaby she remembered hearing at some long-ago time. Her voice broke and warbled a bit, but she persevered, then sang the song again as Noelle drifted into a satisfied sleep.

Whispering her daughter's name reminded Abby that she needed to apply for a birth certificate for the little girl. She'd start a list of things to do. And confirm with Maisie that the Seligs' extra room might be a good place for her. The last thing she wanted was to be a burden to the Barlows. It seemed that suddenly she had become a burden to everyone she knew. Besides the Barlow sisters, she was making it difficult for Joel to make the right decision. And she was surely a bother to Cal, who apparently couldn't stand babies, and was met with Noelle at every turn. One step at a time, she would figure this out. But, she had to admit, she'd need help.

———

When she went to the dining room several hours later to fill her water bottle, Abby met Matt, seated at the table.

"Hi, Matt. You've been so busy lately we've hardly seen you. How are things with the pageant?"

He pulled out a chair for her, then sat back in his chair and ran his hands over his face. "Funny you should ask. We are nearly finished setting up the seller's stalls around the square, and the nativity scene in Jerry's barn. And now, everyone is backing out."

"Oh no. It's only two days away. What happened?"

"A number of things. 'Joseph and Mary' have to go tend to her sick mom in Wisconsin, new baby and all. They left today. A whole family of 'fish and fabric sellers' are down with strep throat, and the weather forecast is turning cold. And, the Barlow sisters don't want to be the innkeepers who send away Mary and Joseph."

"That is bad news. What can you do?" Abby wondered if this inn-keeper thought had spurred the sisters to think about turning away hotel business because she and Noelle were taking up valuable space.

"We're making lists of people, tapping shoulders, calling, texting, begging."

"I wish you lots of luck. This project sounds worth doing. Wish I could help but I don't have much to offer right now."

"No worries." Matt's smile brightened his face. "Nice that you asked how it was going, though. Sometimes it seems like Reverend Selig and I are the only ones into it."

Abby gathered her hair in her hand and threw it over her shoulder. "I, for one—for two—plan to take in as much of it as possible." She gave him a warm smile, but his face dimmed. What had she said wrong?

Matt shook his head, as if to clear his thoughts. "Sorry, Abby. You just then reminded me of my wife, Ginny. She had long, curly red hair and adorable freckles, and she used to gather her hair just like that." He blew out a breath and smiled again. "A pleasant memory for sure, but sometimes it pinches."

"I'm sorry, Matt. How long since she passed?"

"About seven years." He slapped his knees. "Well, time for me to hit the hay. Lots to do in the next two days. If you hear of anyone looking for a position in any capacity for the pageant, please let me know."

"I will."

He left the dining room and Abby moved through to the kitchen doorway, where she saw a new water bottle standing ready for her. How would she manage to do all this on her own? "Get a grip, Abby," she scolded herself. "You can do this and you will do this."

"Any chance you'd have a full-time job for me, Bear?" Joel leaned over the engine of the police car as Bear fiddled with the insides. "I've worked as a mechanic in the summers for five years."

Joel knew Bear heard, but the big man did not respond until he'd lowered the hood into place with a slam.

"How about you drive this here car onto the lot so's I can bring in another vehicle? Just park it there beside my pickup." He tossed Joel the keys. "You look like you could use a cup of java and a listening ear. I'm goin' to fetch us some fresh coffee, and you know that don't happen very often around here."

Joel's temptation to smirk was overcome by the heaviness of his heart. Even the chance to drive a cop car a few yards couldn't distract him from his difficulties. He parked the car and headed for Bear's office, not expecting the fresh coffee to be much better than the usual poison. It didn't matter when one's plans and dreams were on the line.

Before he got to the office door, Bear met him, gesturing to his pickup truck. "Let's go. Sol's always got a fresh pot on."

"How could I be so lucky?" Joel's remark earned him a fake frown from Bear.

When they entered the bistro, Sol Wuppertal met them with a grin and a salute. "This is a new one on me," he said. "Either Bear really likes you, or he's afraid another quaff of his tar will finally start to affect his health."

"Bring us whatever you got." Bear took one of the soft leather chairs that flanked the fireplace and gestured to Joel to take the other. "It's a little before afternoon rush, so we should have some privacy."

Joel eased into the other chair and relaxed. No point in letting his anxiety leap out of bounds. He needed to think aloud about his decision, and who better to listen than Bear, the man of unexpected wisdom.

"Lay it on me, brother." Bear nodded his thanks when Sol brought their drinks, and settled back in his comfy chair.

Joel believed Bear cared about him. It was nice to be accepted and listened to without the immediate judgment he'd come to expect from people...like his father. He took a sip of the excellent half-sweet gingerbread latte and looked off into the distance. Sometimes it was too hard to meet a person's eyes. "I thought I had made a decision yesterday, but today it's flipping to the other side of the fence again. Maybe if I lay it out, you can help me put it to rest. One way or another, I need to move forward."

Bear said nothing, just sat and sipped his coffee.

"See, I've had this dream for years of becoming a doctor. I worked summers as a mechanic, as I told you, to save money for medical college. Any extra time I had was spent at the volunteer medical clinic in a nearby city, gaining experience and knowledge.

"With all the challenges Abby has faced lately, I decided I could not leave her alone, without even a home to go to. I was okay with that, because I had no specific plans for medical studies. Even after all my submissions, I had not received any acceptances to college. I thought I'd accompany Abby back home where life was familiar, and help her get back on her feet. Or, as she seems to be thinking the past couple of days, stay here in Happenstance and help her get settled. Maybe I could get a job with you?"

He stopped for a sip of his coffee and looked to Bear for a hint of his thoughts.

The big man nodded. "Keep talkin', kid. Sometimes you gotta get it all out there, you know?"

"Yeah, so then yesterday, I got this letter in the mail. I had emailed my parents to tell them where I was, and they must

71

have forwarded the letter. It found me way out here in the middle of nowhere! From my first-choice college. An acceptance for me to begin my studies right after the new year. That's, like, a week away."

"Crazy," said Bear. "Every year that new year starts right after the old one ends."

Joel chuckled. "You think they'd give you a bit of lead time to transition, right?"

Bear nodded sagely, then continued to sip.

"What do I do now? Funny, that's what Abby asked me the other day. 'What do I do now?' She's never asked me or anyone for help before. I always told myself I'd stick with her because...because..."

"Because you love her."

"Yeah." Joel glanced around him but none of the few patrons were within listening distance. "And now this comes up. My dream about to come true, and I'm going to pass it up to stay in Happenstance?"

"It ain't all that bad, you know. Nice place to visit or to stay."

"It's not that, Bear. But even though I thought I'd made up my mind that Abby and Noelle come first, I'm having second thoughts."

Bear sat forward, set his cup on the little table between them, and spoke. "First of all, did Abby ask you to stay here and help her?"

"No. But she doesn't know what to do."

"Does she know about your dream of becoming a doctor?"

"Yes."

"What aren't you tellin' me?"

With a deep sigh, Joel replied. "She said to chase my dream, that she'd be fine and I'd better not give it another thought."

"Aha. But you put on your Robert Hood cape and rode in on your white horse to save her."

Joel stared at Bear. "Huh?"

Sol, who had approached to top up their drinks with some regular coffee, interpreted. "He most likely means Robin Hood, who didn't ride a white charger, but ran around Nottingham Forest on his own two green-shod feet.

Otherwise, the meaning is similar. In a way. If you'll excuse me." He backed away, his eyebrows raised.

"Ignore him," said Bear. "Now, where were we?"

"I'm not sure," said Joel. "Something about Robert— Robin Hood."

"Oh yeah. There's somethin' about women, Joel, that you gotta remember. They say they don't know what to do, but that don't mean they want you to tell them what to do, or to do it for them."

"They don't?"

"Nope. What they want is for you to listen and at least pretend to understand."

"You're kidding."

"True stuff, kid."

"Then what?"

"Then you tell 'em they can do this, whatever it is, that they got what it takes and they'll be fine, and if they ever need you, you'll come chargin' to the rescue on that white horse Sol don't believe in. If they need you."

The guy had a point. The day after Abby had told him she didn't know what to do, she'd begun collecting baby supplies as if she had a plan. Even a half-baked one. She'd never mentioned her Aunt Eve again. "Then I need to support her, but carry on with my own plan?"

"You can tell her you'll give up your dream for her, but I know what she's gonna say."

"She already did. But she didn't seem that sure, nor am I, the longer I think about it."

"Course she ain't sure. Life don't come with no guarantees. But she is willin' to try."

Although Bear's words made sense, Joel didn't feel at peace with leaving. He told Bear what he thought.

"You gotta follow your gut, kid. Just let me know if you're still lookin' for a job in my shop, cuz you been a tremendous help the last week, and you got it if you need it."

"Will do. And thanks for listening, Bear. Means a lot to me." Joel had hoped the problem would be solved, but the facts had become more tangled in his mind. Maybe instead of one or the other, there were other options he needed to think about. Maybe...

As they stood from their chairs, a gruff voice carried to them from the lending library on the other side of the half-wall. "You'd best listen to this wise man." The voice belonged to Morris Craddock, who Joel had met briefly. "After all, who has more experience or expertise with women than Gavin Beresford, who has never been married? We don't even know if he's ever been out on a date. Doesn't even have a sister."

"Thanks for the vote of confidence, Morris," said Bear dryly.

"No problem. Have a nice day."

When Bear jumped into his truck to return to his shop, Joel waved and set out walking back to the hotel. He needed time to think.

Chapter 9

When Abby heard the main doors of the hotel open and close, she checked on Noelle, then hurried down the long hall to meet Joel. She broke into a smile. "Joel! You'll never guess what happened this morning." She realized she was being the butterfly he sometimes referred to. Better tamp it down a bit. But her brief time with Maisie this morning had given her more encouragement to make a move.

Joel wore a determined look on his face, and she wondered at the cause of it.

"Let's have a coffee in the parlor where we can talk...if you have time," she suggested.

"As you wish," he said, returning her smile.

His response bothered her. Butterfly was one thing, but Buttercup was quite another. *The Princess Bride* allusion bothered her.

Sure enough, the tea table in the parlor held two cups of steaming coffee, along with the usual bonus, this time a small bowl of trail mix.

"A person could get spoiled living here." Joel spooned some nuts and dried fruit pieces into his hand and tossed them into his mouth.

"That's what I'm worried about." Abby sipped her exquisite coffee, gesturing around her. "If I stay here much longer, I'll become so reliant I won't be able to manage on my own."

Joel gazed at her. "Why would you have to manage on your own? I don't intend to abandon you at a time when your whole life is changing."

"But Joel..." Abby stood to pace. She needed air, movement, something. He was reading her mind and she mustn't let him. "Taking advantage of the opportunity of a lifetime is not abandonment. We've already decided you will go to college immediately, so you're there for opening classes."

"We have? I don't remember confirming any plans."

She almost stamped her foot. Usually, Joel placated her, went along with her wishes, although she rarely asked him to do anything outright. He'd always been nearby when she needed to talk, to confide, to rant, or just needed company. "You cannot miss out on this training. It's what you've been preparing for all your life."

"Have I?"

He was infuriating. "Joel! Stop this. Be the friend you've always been to me."

"Sit down and listen."

Stiff-shouldered, she eased into the chair across from him. "But I..."

"Please, Abby. I've given this some thought. There are other ways, other times to get my training. Right now, you and Noelle are most important. The present comes first, then the future will unfold as it should."

"You sound all new-agey like my parents."

"No. Not at all like them. It's a matter of trusting that if I do the right thing now—that means helping you and Noelle— God will provide for my future."

Abby leaned forward and poked her finger into his chest. "Noelle and I are not your responsibility." She saw the hurt in his eyes and hurried to explain herself. "What I mean is you don't have to put your life on hold for us."

"That's it? I'm just a temporary convenience?"

"Joel, don't put words in my mouth. I want the best for you."

"And you think you know what that is?"

This conversation was getting out of hand. "I should go check on Noelle." As she swept out of the room, she heard him call.

"Bring her back here and tell me what happened this morning."

Abby kissed Noelle and talked with her as she changed her diaper, then washed up and, determined to hear him out, headed back to where Joel waited in the parlor. When she walked in, he was standing at the window, lost in his thoughts, in his resolve, whatever that was.

He turned when he heard them and reached for Noelle. "Hi sweetie," he crooned, and Abby saw the love in his eyes.

On one hand, how could he not love this little angel? On the other, how could he love a child who was not even his? Whose father was his ex-best friend?

Joel nestled Noelle into his neck, then moved nearer to Abby. "Please don't take this away from me. I know she's not mine, nor are you, but I can't seem to give up on either of you. It's like the interruption that changes your life, you know?"

Lowering her head, Abby whispered, "Yes, I do know. I've always taken what comes, but this time, it's all too big to simply accept and move on. It's a full stop."

Their gazes locked, and she had to physically back away to break eye contact. She'd never before experienced this feeling of reality. Her life had been a dream, sometimes good, sometimes bad, but a kind of story. One she could shape to her own ending. Or just walk away and start a new chapter. Now she was at a crossroads. No, she'd crossed the road already, into a new life. No walking away. What a puzzle life could be.

Noelle squeaked, and Joel patted her, talking to her in his earnest way as he walked the carpet. "Abby, tell me what you were excited about when I came back just now. You have some news, I think."

"Oh yeah. I do." She set aside the intense feelings that swirled through her. "Maisie had some free time today, and offered to come with me to see the Seligs. About a place to stay."

She looked to Joel but he didn't reply, just nodded for her to continue. "I can't keep taking up space here when the Barlow sisters need the income from their hotel. And a baby on the premises isn't the best way to encourage guests to return."

"What did the Seligs say?"

"They're open to having me...us...I mean, Noelle and me, stay with them. They have three bedrooms in the parsonage, one for them, one for the reverend's study, and an extra. It's at the end of the hallway right next to the bathroom, and they have an ensuite in their room, so we wouldn't put each other out. Except if Noelle decides to cry a lot. Which she hasn't thus far. What do you think?"

"You're asking me?"

"I just did."

"How much are they asking for rent, and do you have a way of earning any money?"

Always the details. But Abby knew she had to start thinking practically now that she was a mother. "I'm not sure yet. They said if I helped around the house and yard, I could stay for free. If and when I get a job, I would begin to pay rent."

"Sounds more than fair to me. Where would you work?"

"Not sure. Maisie offered me part time laundering her towels and sweeping up at the salon, maybe even doing some books. But I'd have to bring Noelle with me, and that involves a few more expenses like a swing and a playpen, stuff like that."

Joel shook his head, and she was afraid he would bring up some negative points she had overlooked. Instead, he marveled at the kindness of the people in Happenstance. "Bear said I could work for him if I decided to stay in town, but I haven't considered a place to stay yet."

"You're sure, then? That you're staying?"

"Yes, unless you tell me to hit the road."

"I did, but you didn't listen."

He grinned, sat down on the sofa with Noelle, and began to talk to her. The little girl listened as if she understood, and Abby's heart soared. How could she push him away? For now, why not accept his offer and his help? She'd have to think about his "as you wish," but he was definitely growing on her. Unlike Ricky, who had bailed at the first sign of a speed bump in the road.

Noelle had fallen asleep to the soft sound of Joel's voice, and he offered to take her back to her room. On his way, he asked if Abby would like to go for a short walk.

"What about Noelle? The monitor doesn't have much range."

"I'll see if I can access it through my phone. Besides, we'd only be gone about ten minutes or so."

That done, they left the hotel, with Abby casting glances over her shoulder until they were out on the lane.

"Let's walk to the end of the lane and back," Joel suggested. "You could probably use some fresh air."

Without thinking about it, Abby linked her arm through

Joel's, and they strolled together like the friends they used to be, and thankfully, still were.

Chapter 10

Cal couldn't believe what she saw. Both Abby and Joel strolling along the lane together, arm in arm, with no thought whatsoever to the helpless baby alone in that large room at the end of the corridor. Did they have no care at all for their child?

She would never do that, leave a baby alone. You never knew what could happen. She'd have to keep watch, listen, make sure all was okay. Thank goodness Sandy didn't need her today, it being a Saturday. She had no idea what he did on his days off; they didn't talk much. And she didn't really want to know. Best to stay out of the loop, out of circulation as much as possible. She didn't need or want anyone keeping track of her.

It was a relief that Sandy didn't push, didn't question, just left her alone with her own thoughts. That wasn't necessarily good though, she had to admit. Not at all. Her thoughts were her greatest enemies during the day, dark and brooding. And she didn't even want to think about the nightmares. Maybe she should go for a walk too, although then the baby would be completely alone. No, she couldn't do that.

Cal walked quietly along the hallway, then heard the baby squeak. She was waking up. Alone. This would never do. When were those kids coming back to their responsibilities? Who did they expect would take care of the child while they were away? Angels? Cal snorted. As if. Just like... No! She shut down her thoughts, pushed them back into the shadows of her mind. And took action.

"You're right about a walk in the fresh air doing me good." Abby felt lighter as they climbed the steps to the hotel and let themselves inside.

"I'm going to run up to my room for a few minutes," said Joel. "See you at dinner. And thanks for the walk."

That look again. Abby felt drawn to him as she never had before. Maybe, just maybe... She smiled. "I'll go check on Noelle and see you later."

He squeezed her hand and leapt up the stairs two at a time. Grinning, she sauntered along the hallway toward her room, then hesitated at the open door. Had someone checked on Noelle and forgotten to close it?

Pushing it open, she glanced in, and not seeing Noelle in her crib, looked around the room. No one was there. Instantly on alert, she ran from the room and into the parlor, thinking she may have missed someone sitting there with Noelle. Empty.

She poked her head into the dining room, even knocked on the door to the kitchen. When Johanna appeared, her face dusted with flour, Abby asked if anyone had been by with the baby.

"No. You must look."

A sudden thought hit Abby like a kick in the gut. Could Cal have taken Noelle? She had the opportunity. But why? She avoided babies. Well, she avoided both Abby and Noelle when they were together. Maybe it was Abby herself that Cal was avoiding, for some unknown reason.

"Joel!" She ran toward the entrance, calling his name.

He met her at the bottom of the stairs. "What's up? Where's Noelle?"

"I don't know. She's gone. What do we do? Where do we look?" She clung to his arm, too tense for tears. "I shouldn't have left. I have to find her."

"I'll help you." He whipped out his phone. "Bear, we have an incident. Abby and I were just outside for a few minutes, and now Noelle is missing. We need help."

"Take a breath, Joel. I'm on my way."

Emmaline poked her head out of her room and hurried to where Abby and Joel were talking. "What's going on?"

"Noelle is missing," said Abby, feeling her stomach burning. "She's just gone."

"What? How can that be?"

"I don't know. We have to go find her."

"Grayce and I will pray. The good Lord knows where your baby is." And she was gone to find her sister.

Joel's voice interrupted Abby. "Bear's on his way."

She ran toward the entrance door.

"Wait, Abby. You need a coat. And you won't get far on

foot. I can hear Bear's old truck. He'll be here in a minute."

"I'll get my coat. Where is it?"

"Abby." Joel grabbed her shoulders. "We can't fly apart. We need to keep our heads. Let's get our coats and meet back here. Bear's already coming up the lane."

She flew along the hallway to her room and grabbed the coat she'd borrowed from Maisie, along with the hat, scarf and mitts. When Emmaline reappeared with Grayce by her side, Abby didn't stop. "No time to talk. Bear is here to help us find Noelle."

She ran to meet Joel at the door, and he pulled her outside toward Bear's truck.

Bear leaned over and threw open the door of his truck. "It's gonna be cozy, but it's the best I got."

The kids looked panicked, just as he would have been in their situation. "Now calm down, you two. I been havin' a conversation with the Lord, and worry ain't gonna help."

"But my Noelle," said Abby. "It's getting dark outside and it's too cold for her. She only a week old!"

Abby climbed into Bear's old half-ton, moving close so there would be room for Joel. "Let's go."

"Hold up, Abby," said Bear. "We need at least a basic plan."

He felt Abby's terror rise as she leveled a hard look at him. "Please, let's just go."

With a sigh, Bear put his truck into gear and headed out along the lane, onto Main Street North, and around the oval. They checked out pedestrians as well as cars, which were few on the street at this time of day.

Bear sent Joel a look that begged for help. This chugging along the streets wasn't doing the trick at all.

Then Abby burst out, "It's her! It's that Cal woman!"

"What?" Bear slowed and studied the street. "Where?"

"I don't know where she is, but I'm sure she did it," roared Abby. "She took my baby. Who else would have? Matt isn't home today, Sandy's been off somewhere since morning, the ladies were napping in their rooms, and Johanna is baking something. Only Cal could have done it."

Bear glanced at the road, then back at the freaked out young woman.

"If not Cal, then who? Some weirdo off the street? In Happenstance?"

Before Bear could give Joel the eye, the kid put his arm around Abby and held her tightly. "It's okay, Abby. We're on our way. Keep praying and let God handle this."

"Good advice, Joel, my man. I'm thinkin' God's got more goin' on here than any of us knows."

Abby shook off Joel's arm. Not a good sign.

"Listen, Abby," said Joel. "What are you saying? Why would Cal take Noelle? You've told me yourself, she doesn't get anywhere near her."

Bear felt the electricity in the cab of his truck. Best keep his mouth shut unless he had something important to say.

"Maybe it's not Noelle she's been avoiding. Maybe it's me. And I wasn't there with Noelle. I was outside getting some air, of all the dumb ideas. How could I have been so stupid, leaving my baby inside while that woman was there?"

Bear leaned forward and gave Joel a questioning look.

Joel nodded back to him. "You might be right, Abby. But where would she go? She doesn't know anyone here."

"Maybe to the bistro. I saw her when Maisie and I were there. She was wearing a hat and scarf to cover her hair, but I knew it was her."

"Ooh, boy." Bear swung around and parked in front of the bistro. Joel and Abby piled out and disappeared into the building while he kept the truck running. As quick as lightning, they were back, pushing their way into the vehicle.

"Not there." Abby's words were now drowning in terror. She clung to Joel's arm.

Without a plan, Bear backed out of the parking space and began to weave through town, looking for clues. He knew there had to be a better way, but he'd allowed Abby to push him.

Joel's cellphone rang. "Hello? Miss Emmaline. No. Oh. Good to know. Thank you. Yes, please."

"What did she say," demanded Abby.

"They thought of Cal too. They checked her room—the chapel—and she wasn't there, nor was any of her stuff."

"And?"

"They're going to keep praying."

"Oh great! We need action, not prayers."

Bear got a brainwave. "Call Sandy. He knows her favorite places we wouldn't know about."

Joel pulled out his phone again, and once getting Sandy, told him the story. He reported as he stuck the phone back into his pocket. "He says, meet him at the park entrance. He has an idea."

"The park?" Abby turned on Joel. "Why would she take my baby to the park? That's just stupid."

Nevertheless, Bear whipped his truck around toward Lakeview Forest and stepped on the gas.

They rolled into the parking lot of Lakeview Forest, and there stood Sandy, waiting for them. "Huh," said Bear, "must be the first time I didn't have to go searchin' him out."

They pushed out of the truck and ran up to Sandy, who put a finger to his lips and beckoned them to follow him. The sun had begun to sink, and the coming darkness descended as they entered the trees. Bear took up position at the back of the group, heading for a place Sandy had in mind. At least he hoped Sandy had an idea where he was going.

Chapter 11

As they trudged through the snow farther into the trees, Bear felt the quiet descend. The breeze could barely be felt this deep, and the animals must have settled in for the night, at least the diurnal ones. Even the birds were still.

Poor Noelle. Where was she? Was she safe from creatures? Did Cal have her, and if so, where? She must have taken her; Noelle couldn't have gone off on her own. None of Bear's questions had answers. Poor Abby must be ready to break. He'd have to keep his eye on her if they met up with Cal out here. Abby was liable to tackle her and beat her up. He sent up more prayers for protection all around.

They stopped walking when Sandy held up a hand. "Wait here," he whispered. Joel held Abby, and Bear stood behind them like their own private protector.

Sandy moved forward and edged around a small clearing, as far as Bear could see. Then he disappeared behind some trees, and suddenly, the space lit up like a Christmas tree. It was a Christmas tree...or rather, many. White lights lit up the clearing like stars in the sky.

And in the light, Cal sat in the center of the nativity scene, cuddling a baby.

"Noelle!" Abby broke away and ran toward them, but Sandy got there first. He gently lifted the baby from Cal's arms and turned toward Abby. She held Noelle to her chest and cried, shaking with grief and relief. Joel stood with her, rubbing her back, soothing them both with a soft voice.

At the hubbub, Noelle began to wail, and Bear grinned. "She's okay," he said. "That's a mad wail, if I'm right."

Sandy knelt before Cal and took her hands. "What ye be doin', love? Why ye be takin' someone's bairn away? These be worried sick."

Cal raised her face to look at Noelle, then back to Sandy. "They left her all alone, Sandy. Poor little Sheera was all alone. She started to cry and I had to take care of her because they left her. She wasn't safe there. That girl doesn't know how to take care of a child."

"At least I don't take her out in the middle of the winter, into the forest." Abby's voice was loud and angry. Joel kept a firm hold on her. "I know how to care for my own child. What do you know about children anyway?"

Sandy glanced at Bear, bewilderment on his face. Bear moved in and suggested Sandy take the little family home where it was warm and dry. He saw a pile of wood that either Cal or Sandy had gathered, and made a small fire, tending it carefully.

Sandy led the others away, to his vehicle, to the way back to the warm, cozy hotel.

"Come sit nearer the fire," Bear said to Cal as he pulled a large log near the blaze. He sat down and after a few moments, Cal moved closer and held out her hands to the fire.

Then she lowered her head into her hands and sobbed. "I got mixed up. I thought it was Sheera crying and she was all alone. And when she cried, I could hear Benji and Belle screaming for me, but I couldn't get to them. I was safe at home, and they were dying. And my Gabe couldn't help them because he was already dead." She wailed then, choking on her sorrow.

Shock hit Bear as he tried to follow her mumbled words, then he moved close to Cal and put his arm around her. "It's okay, Callie girl. You take your time to remember and I'll be here. I won't leave you."

She leaned into him and cried brokenheartedly until Bear's own heart broke at her pain. He reached out and threw more wood on the fire to keep it going, and then he began to talk.

"Don't you worry, Callie girl. Your family, they're safe with Jesus now. Whatever happened, he never left them alone. And your Gabe...was he your husband?"

She nodded and wiped her face on her sleeve.

With southern manners, Bear fished a clean hanky from his pocket and gave it to her. "Why don't you tell me about him?"

Cal snuffled and hiccupped. "He...he and I got married right out of college. He was such a good dad..." She cried some more, than seemed to get hold of herself. "He adored the kids. Three of them. Benji and Belle were twins, so we had a bang-up introduction to parenthood."

She shook all over and Bear kept his arms around her until she settled a bit.

"When the twins were two, we had another baby. We called her Sheera. Can you believe it? Three kids under the age of three? All I did was care for the kids. Gabe worked at his job, ran home at lunch to help out, then after dinner he cooked and cleaned and helped me not to lose my mind. Day after day. We were a team, even though he carried most of the burden of kids and a wife."

After a long, heavy silence, Bear asked, "What happened to them?"

"Car accident. All gone in minutes." Again, Cal buried her face in his flannel jacket and sobbed. When she'd calmed some, she told him. The crackle of the fire filled the silence. All Bear could think to say was, "I'm sorry. So very sorry. I'm here."

She glanced up at him and reached up to wipe the tears from his cheeks, then settled once again into his hug. The fire died and she began to shiver, both from her relived trauma and from the descending cold, Bear guessed.

"We're gonna go back where you can get warmed up and have a good sleep, okay, Callie girl?"

"He called me that, you know? Gabe called me his Callie girl."

"I'm sorry, Cal. I won't—"

"No, don't apologize. I love to hear my real name again. It's such a comfort not to be called Cal and be thought of as a cold, horrible woman. But I suppose I am horrible. What a major, unforgiveable screw-up."

"I'd never think that of you. A few more piercings and tattoos than I'm used to, but I can adapt."

Callie snorted, then sobered. "The vine is for Gabe, reminding me how his love once encircled me. The three ear piercings are for my babies."

"And the eyebrow rings?"

She heaved a sigh. "Also for the kids. And for pain. If I feel physical pain, I don't feel the jagged edges of my heart as much. Silly, I know."

"No, it's not. But it doesn't help. Does it?"

"No. Bear?"

"Yeah?"

"I'm about as frozen as a snowman."

He kicked himself for being obtuse. "Of course. I'm sorry. Let's go." He pushed some snow onto the fire with his boot and stomped it out.

"Where can I go? I can't face Abby."

"I know just the place. Let's wander on outta here—do you know how to turn off these lights?—and we'll be there soon."

"Sandy had it hooked up back here somewhere." Callie disappeared behind the biggest evergreen and after a couple of minutes, the lights went out. "Bear? You still here?"

"Course I am, Callie girl. Right here."

She bumped into him, then claimed his hand, and together they headed out of Lakeview Forest and eventually to his truck.

"I'll get this thing goin' and the heater will be blazin' in a instant."

"I didn't mean to hurt her, you know. The baby. She was alone. Her mama's gonna kill me, isn't she?"

"Naw. I won't let her do that. You were protectin' the little one. Come on, now."

They drove across Bridgeway Avenue and turned into the church parking lot. He pulled up close to the parsonage and went around to open her door. "C'mon, Callie. I'm gonna introduce you to two of the nicest people in Happenstance."

Abby woke with a start and pushed herself up in bed. "Noelle!"

In the soft glow of a night light, Joel whispered from the rocking chair. "Noelle is fine, Abby. She's sleeping in her bassinet right beside you."

Abby reached out and gently felt the form of her sleeping child. Why was Joel sitting in her room? In the middle of the night? Then she remembered. He had refused to leave her side. He had given her time to change into pajamas and crawl into her bed before appearing again with a pillow and blanket. He'd settled into the rocking chair and vowed he would not leave.

What a dear friend. No, he was much more than a friend. He was here for her as he had promised. For her and Noelle. She lay back in bed, her arms behind her head, and said thank you to the One who Joel said had protected them all this night.

She sat up again. "Joel?"

He straightened, ready to get whatever she needed, she was sure.

"Thank you." She blew him a kiss, smiled and fell back into a welcoming sleep.

Callie sat in the Seligs' cozy kitchen with a mug of hot chocolate in her hands and a blanket around her shoulders.

The Seligs had been visiting quietly around the table with Bear, about the snow, the temperature, and the Christmas pageant. None of them pressed her for details, and she gradually warmed up, but she couldn't stop shaking. She knew she had some tall explaining to do, and maybe a jail sentence coming up for her erratic behavior, but right now, all she needed was the soothing timbre of Bear's voice and the warm chocolate sliding down her throat.

She took a last swallow of the hot milk, then became aware of the silence around her. Setting down the mug, she cleared her throat. Time to 'fess up. Again.

Reverend Selig reached a hand across the table. "How about my Annaliese brings you a bit of soup and a fresh roll, and when you've eaten, you can crawl into bed and sleep until you're not tired anymore?"

"But you don't even...I just...you'd let me stay here after all that's happened?"

"You need a place," said Annaliese, standing to pat her shoulder, "and we have here more than we need. I will get soup."

Bear patted Callie's other shoulder. "These dear people will keep watch over you for the night, and Annaliese invited me for breakfast tomorrow. I'm lookin' forward to that! For now, that's enough. We can talk more tomorrow. Okay?"

"Okay." She smiled in relief. "I'm so tired I can hardly remember my name."

"It's Callie," said Bear. "I ain't forgettin' that any time

soon. Now let's ask the reverend to pray with us, and then I'm gonna go check on my trailer. Got me a cat, and she will be some upset if I don't feed her soon."

A smile pulled at Callie's lips. How could she smile with all she'd been through? What she'd put everyone else through? But she smiled. There was a comfort that couldn't be expressed, and she would accept it and carry on tomorrow.

The reverend prayed a comforting prayer, and Annaliese set a bowl of warm vegetable soup before her. Bear pushed back his chair and left with a nod that carried more meaning than she could decipher right now.

"Thanks for everything, Bear. All of you. I feel wrapped in love right now, and I don't deserve it."

"We'll talk about that more another day," said the reverend. "You have enough to process. You will no doubt be facing police interviews and court proceedings and psychiatric tests. Those are the facts. But you must also remember that you are not alone, and although neither you nor I nor anyone deserves the love of God, His love is another of the inescapable facts. Those of us who are getting to know you will stand by you through whatever is required."

She received another pat on the shoulder from Annaliese, and the soup, although she had thought she didn't have an appetite, soothed her. Exhaustion overtook her soon after she crawled into the soft, flannel sheets of the cozy bed at the end of the hallway.

Abby definitely had some thinking to do. She could do that now that she had Noelle cuddled to her chest. She sat in the parlor, a cup of steaming lemon tea with honey at her elbow. The fire burned in the grate, encouraging contemplation.

Her world had been rocked when Cal had taken Noelle. She thought her heart would explode, and she was so glad to get her baby back that she hadn't vented all the anger inside. She wanted to, but the reverend had just paid her a visit.

He was a kind man, but no old geezer, as she'd first thought. None of these people were, well, except maybe Morris at the bistro, but she had a feeling he only put on an act.

But Reverend Selig was straight up. He didn't beat around the bush, but said what he meant and meant what he said. The difference between him and some other preacher-types Abby had met in her life was that his words were cloaked with love. He actually cared about her. And Noelle. And Joel.

The thing she had to consider was that he also cared about Cal—or Callie, as she was now known. In fact, Callie was staying at the parsonage right now. The fact that Abby didn't have to see Callie every day gave her some peace, but she'd been thinking further. Joel would laugh if she told him. Or maybe not. Abby had never been one to plan ahead. But that was before she became a mother.

She'd been seriously thinking that it would be better for Callie to stay with the Seligs than for her and Noelle. I mean, Callie needed professional help. When Abby heard the story of her multiple losses, she began to understand how that could put a person over the top. Just the wrong stressors and she'd be back at the time of the accident. PTSD for sure.

As long as Callie got help, Abby was okay having her in the same town. But she needed to find a place for herself and Noelle. No ideas had come yet. Not surprising, since she'd only been in Happenstance just over a week. And, with Christmas coming, most people weren't ready to think about inviting someone—with a baby—into their homes to live.

The reverend had prayed with her that things would fall into place as they should, but Abby was still wondering where it would all end up. Although, there was little she could do about it right now. Maybe she'd lean her head into the pillows and doze off. Noelle was doing that, so no better time.

Abby looked out the window of the Seligs' living room, smiling at the glistening snow. It was the day before Christmas Eve, and she'd come for a friendly visit, since Bear had taken Callie to Athens to see a counselor.

Abby had told the Seligs her thoughts about Callie staying with them, and they had agreed. "Very kind it is of you to give her this opportunity," said Annaliese, "in spite of what she did. You are growing up, my dear."

The visit with the Seligs was just what Abby needed, and she felt somewhat better, having followed her heart by offering the promised room to Callie. No, the woman didn't deserve it, but then, she hadn't deserved to lose her family either. Abby could not imagine how that would feel, how a person could live a normal life after a traumatic experience like that. Knowing helped her understand Callie and what she'd done. Although it sure didn't excuse it.

Also, the reverend explained to her that no one deserved anything good, but because God was good, he loved to bless his people. It was more than Abby could fathom, but she felt she'd begun a journey. She didn't have to have it all figured out at once.

They had also talked about the Living Nativity. Almost everything was set. The weather station altered their predictions to include sunshine and cheery temperatures through Christmas. Hopefully, that wouldn't change last minute.

"All we need is a Mary and Joseph," said Reverend Selig. "The other positions are all filled now. And a camel would be nice!"

"Who is the innkeeper? The Barlows did not want to be the ones to turn away the Christ Child."

Annaliese answered her question. "They have reconsidered, yes?"

The reverend smiled. "The Barlows are precious."

"I know." Abby kissed the top of Noelle's downy head. "They've been kind to me, as have many others, including you two."

"We are most happy to help." Annaliese reached over and squeezed Abby's hand.

She is a delightful old soul, thought Abby, and very aware of what goes on around her. In fact, Abby's opinion of older folks had changed a lot since she and Joel had blown into Happenstance such a short time ago.

Sometimes the realities of life are harder when you choose to face them, but the joys of accomplishing new things and taking life in hand is worth it.

Without thinking, she said, "I loved it here. Everyone was nice, supportive. A perfect little town. Until Callie took my baby."

Annaliese nodded, but looked to her husband.

"Abby," he said, "you know this is not a perfect town. There are good people here, many of them, but I'm afraid evil exists, in any dark corner where it's given a foothold. Even in those who don't realize what they're doing. We must learn to trust in the Lord for each day. He is faithful."

Annaliese nodded. "Amen. He is faithful."

Annaliese's confirmation challenged Abby. "But you've lost so much, and I almost lost my sweet baby." She cuddled Noelle close to her chest. They had told her about losing their sweet little girl when she was only five. What a weight to carry. And yet, here they were encouraging her.

The reverend reached over and took his wife's hand. "We had to learn to hold our blessings loosely. We are not promised an easy life, Abby, or even a pleasant one. We are called to give ourselves up to the One who knows the whole story from beginning to end."

Abby didn't want to upset them, but then, they'd probably had similar discussions with other people, being the pastor couple in town. "But how do you trust someone you can't even see? Who is he anyway?"

The Seligs wore matching smiles, but again, she let him do the talking. He picked up a leather-bound book from the coffee table. "This, my dear, is God's love letter to us. It's filled with examples of those who followed and those who didn't. Filled with the story of how he rescued us from the power of sin.

"Our part is to accept his love personally, and get to know him by reading this letter. Do you have a Bible of your own?"

Abby shook her head, dumbfounded by the simple words he used to tell her his version of the truth. "You believe that, but what if I don't?"

Her words did not seem to upset him at all. "It's hard to believe in someone you've never known. I have a Bible for you to take home. I will include a list of special passages to read—there's an index too—and let you find out what it says for yourself. If you have any questions as you go, just ask. We are always happy to help in any way we can."

Reverend Selig gave Abby a ride back to the hotel in time

for lunch. Joel wasn't back yet; he was hard at work helping Matt and other volunteers pull together the setup and backdrops for the many sites of the Living Nativity. She wanted to hear his take on what the reverend and Annaliese had told her. She had never bothered to ask Joel before what he believed. That was one of those personal things she thought was none of her business. Now she wanted Joel's feedback on it. Also, she had a couple of great ideas for the Nativity event.

Chapter 12

Joel and Matt laughed and talked as the group ate the delicious potato soup and fresh biscuits served by Johanna.

"Sounds like it's all coming together," said Abby. "The reverend said besides Mary and Joseph, you need a camel!"

"A camel. My word, that's all we need." Grayce frowned. "I know everyone wants this presentation to be at its best, but it already has all the necessary components."

"I'm sure they were joking," said Emmaline. "There aren't any camels for some distance around. Only llamas."

"Not llamas, Emm," corrected Grayce. "Alpacas. They are smaller."

"Alpacas!" Matt slapped the table, bringing everyone to attention. "We should ask Eleanor Burkett if she would let us use a couple of hers for the manger scene."

"I'd love to see them," said Abby. "May I come...never mind. I can't take Noelle into a pasture."

"You go ahead." Joel reached for another biscuit. "I'll watch Noelle. As long as she's fed, we'll be fine."

Abby hesitated, then shook her head. "I can't leave her, Joel."

He stood from the table and led her into the parlor where they wouldn't be overheard. "Listen, Abby. Callie isn't here. Between the Seligs and Bear, they are keeping tabs on her. Don't you think I can care for Noelle?"

"Yes, but she's..."

"She's not mine. I know that. But what you don't seem to understand is that I love her as if she were."

She studied him for long moments, then seemed to come to a conclusion. "Yes, you do love her. It's just...if anything should happen..."

"You'd be ten minutes away, and you have your phone. Please, give yourself a break and let me enjoy Noelle."

Her lips pressed together, she finally nodded. "Okay. I trust you."

"Now try to relax and take this all in. You love animals. It will be fun."

"Yes, it will. Thank you, Joel." She kissed his cheek and turned to go. "Check—"

"I will check on Noelle right away. Now scoot."

She turned back to him once more. "By the way, I think you and I and Noelle could pass for a pretty good holy family, as long as no one checks our credentials!"

Her words shocked Joel. He would never have guessed she'd be willing to be part of the main nativity scene, first, because it was cool and dusty; second, because she didn't know the importance of the event. But he'd take her up on it. "Consider it done," he said. "We'll make sure all the straw bales have been put in place by tonight. The dust can settle, and hopefully, tomorrow will be a beautiful sunny day. The barn doors face the south into the sunshine. Thanks, Abby. I'm glad you suggested this."

As she and Joel re-entered the dining room, she said, "Put your minds at ease. All characters accounted for. If we fit an alpaca with a hump of some kind, we even have our camel."

"Case solved." Matt gave Joel a high five. "You ready to go, Abby?"

"Yes I am."

Just then, Johanna entered with a paper sack for Matt and Abby and a platter for the table. The plate held delicate chocolate meringues, which were no doubt also the contents of the bag. "Freshly made."

"Why, thank you, Johanna," said Emmaline. "You are a treasure."

"Danke." Johanna disappeared before Joel or Matt could thank her.

"How does she—"

Matt cut off Joel's words. "Don't ask. I can't answer, only accept and be grateful." He raised the bag of meringues in a salute. "Off to interview alpacas."

Abby deposited Noelle's tiny form into Joel's arms and stooped to kiss her cheek. Joel's breath hitched at her nearness. He noticed a shared glance and raised eyebrows between the Barlow sisters. They were matchmakers at heart, he was sure. Well, Cupid had certainly shot a Noelle-sized arrow through his heart. That was a start.

Then she turned to accompany Matt to the Burkett farm

while he held Noelle to his heart.

As much as Abby loved being with Noelle, cuddling her and getting to know her, she enjoyed visiting the Burkett farm with Matt. Eleanor lived a short three miles out of town. The drive was only long enough, between bites of chocolate meringues, for Matt to give her a brief summary of Eleanor and her animals.

When they arrived, Matt introduced Abby and Eleanor to each other. The woman met them outside the big, old farmhouse that she and her husband had renovated over the years.

"It always makes me sad to think my husband couldn't enjoy all the work he did, but at least he knew he'd taken care of me," she said.

A natural beauty, she pushed her thick, graying blonde hair behind her ears and smiled with a peace and confidence Abby couldn't understand. "And I have my girls, the alpacas. It's always been a dream of mine."

"Could we see them up close?" Abby was excited by the opportunity.

"Of course," Eleanor agreed. "They are such gorgeous creatures, eyes as big as cartoon characters, hair as soft as silk. Let's go see what the girls are up to."

As Eleanor had said, the alpacas, which she introduced as Alice, Belle, Cassie, Deirdre, Elsa, Fiona and Gabby, were delightful. They stood close to three feet tall at the shoulders, their long necks straight and proud, eyes huge, shaded by eyelashes any model would die for. Eleanor called Gabby to her, and the sweet little baby alpaca—a cria, she called it—allowed Abby to dig her fingers into the rich fawn-colored coat.

"It's not greasy like sheep's wool," said Abby.

"No, that's why it's much nicer to work with."

"Do you have products to sell?"

"Yes, I do. I have them at the house. I mostly sell online. I make sweaters, but also some mitts and cozy socks. Cat toys are taking off right now, so I'll be doing more of those." Eleanor turned to Matt. "What brings you out here on this sunny winter day?"

"A question. I'm sure you've heard about the Living Nativity we're putting on in Happenstance. While we were having lunch at the hotel, we were lamenting that we don't have camels for our nativity..."

"And someone suggested my alpacas." She turned back to her small herd. "What do you think, girls? Any volunteers to add some class to the pageant?" Several of them approached her, and she laughed. "Of course, Gabby won't be left out, and Cassie and Fiona are my other two tamest." She addressed Matt and Abby. "I believe I can come up with three. Would that be sufficient?"

"That would be awesome." Abby grinned as Gabby tried to nibble her fingers. "Do you have a way to transport them to the dairy?"

"Jerry Alkmaar has offered the front of his dairy barn as the stable," explained Matt.

"Gotcha. I have a trailer that I use to take them to shows. When do you want them?"

They discussed the details while Abby moved among the animals, who seemed to accept her as a friend. Eleanor watched Abby's easy manner with the creatures, and theirs with her. "If I ever need someone to look after them for a bit, I know who to call."

"I'd be delighted."

Matt shook Eleanor's hand. "Thanks for giving us the close-up, and for agreeing to bring them in tomorrow. I must get back to town and finish the preparations. I hope you'll take the tour through the series of live scenes tomorrow."

"I surely will. Thanks for including me and my girls. They'll hum about this for a long time."

Once Matt and Abby had driven away, Abby asked, "What did she mean about her alpacas humming about their experiences? Sounded kinda weird."

Matt chuckled. "I've read that when alpacas settle down to sleep at night, they tend to hum, as if they're quietly gossiping about their day while they drift into sleep."

"Too cool. I would love to have some of those cuties."

"They're sweet all right, but it's more of an investment than a hobby. They don't come cheap."

"Oh well, I can always bring Noelle out to Eleanor's to see them when she gets a bit older."

"Sounds as if you have decided to stay with us. That's great."

Abby smiled but fidgeted with the hem of her jacket. "For now, anyway. Since my original plan has evaporated, I have to follow another course. The Seligs offered me a room with them until I get on my feet enough to find work, but now I've given it up to Callie. I think she needs those folks more than I do."

"That's awesome, Abby. They are the dearest people around, and will take good care of her. She'd better be prepared to gain some weight though. Annaliese loves to bake cinnamon rolls and strudel."

"I have no other ideas at this point, but I think it will all work out." She couldn't keep herself from continuing. "I'm used to thinking only of myself, but since Noelle came onto the scene, I've realized others are worth thinking about too." She expected a laugh from Matt, but it didn't come.

"That's great to hear, Abby. Some people never get over themselves. The sooner, the better."

"I'm still looking for another place to live, but I won't rush it. The Barlows assured me we were fine at the hotel for as long as we needed it." Not knowing what else to say, she asked, "Do you have family, Matt? I don't know anything about you except that you're a teacher here in Happenstance, and you're a widower."

A silence descended for a few moments before Matt spoke. "No family to speak of. My parents died when I was young, I was raised by my grandparents, who are deceased, and my wife is gone, as you know. We had no children."

Abby felt heat flood her cheeks. "I'm sorry. I did not mean to pry, or to bring up a difficult subject. One never knows what questions are okay to ask these days."

"No worries," said Matt. "My memories of my grandparents and my Ginny are very precious. They make me smile more than cry, but it's still hard to vocalize their absence and my lack of family."

"You seem to be family to the Barlow sisters. In my observation, they adore you."

He grinned. "They are two of the wittiest, funniest, most caring individuals in town."

She relaxed again, aware of how much joy, comfort and encouragement had come her way since she had landed in Happenstance. Who would have thought a blizzard would be a blessing in disguise? She'd still like to fly out to Florida to see Aunt Eve, but that would have to wait until she earned enough money to make the trip, and until she felt at ease traveling with Noelle. Right now, she would bask in the goodness she had fallen into, and enjoy the first Christmas with her own little angel. And with Joel. She was glad he was staying a while longer, even though she knew his sacrifice was great. And it was for her.

This was the first time she had thought about the true meaning of Christmas, of Jesus and why he came. Her mind and heart were full. This must be why so many people truly loved Christmas.

————

Bear squinted out the dirty window of his office and watched Sandy's old clunker pull onto the lot. He'd kept Sandy's pickup running all the time he'd lived in Happenstance, before he'd gone back to Ireland to finish his studies, and he'd continue as long as the truck was fixable.

He was looking forward to another good chat with Sandy, the one man who never faulted his coffee, at least not to his face, but the figure that jumped from the truck to the snowy ground was not that of Sandy Fitzpatrick III.

Bear opened the door and Callie blew in.

"Hey, Bear. Thought I'd come see how you spend your time while Sandy and I are busy counting and categorizing trees."

"And you find me sippin' coffee."

"It's your business. Do what you want. Would you have time to look at Sandy's truck?"

"What seems to be the problem with this old faithful?" he asked. "Not enjoyin' the winter?"

Callie raised an eyebrow. "You're the mechanic."

Pointing to the visitor chair, the replacement Matt had brought in from the second-hand store in Athens, Bear shuffled to his own seat.

"See, it's like this," said Bear, relaxing into his own worn chair. "When I go see Dr. Paula, I give her a hint of what I been feelin', a clue to what I'm lookin' for. It's helpful for a mechanic too, saves time for me and money for Sandy."

"It doesn't start well in the morning, even when it's been plugged in."

"Thank you. That's helpful. You pluggin' it into one of the hotel's outside sockets?"

"Yeah." Her head on the side, she looked interested at last. "Why?"

"Simple reason, cuz they don't work. Ain't hooked up no more. In truth, that old claptrack of a vehicle out there is doin' a bang-up job of startin' without bein' connected to a source of power. Remarkable."

"Oh. Then why would Sandy send me in with it?"

Sandy, you old schemer. "You got me. May as well have a cup of java while you're here." He rose and poured one for her and another for himself.

He handed one to her. "Got some white stuff here if you like it pale." He handed her a shaker of coffee whitener.

"I'd rather die, thanks."

He set the stuff on the corner of his desk and watched her response once she'd tasted his brew. His new machine had slowly become a sludge pot just as his old ones had been. Matt told him to clean it once in a while, but he never got to it.

Callie took a swig, ran to the door and spewed it out onto the gravel of the lot. She poured out the rest. "That stuff is gut rot. How are you still alive, drinking it every day?"

"Hasn't bothered me yet."

"You could pass this stuff off as—"

"Used motor oil. I know, that's what Matt and Joel tell me."

She wiped her lips with the back of her hand and shuddered. He brought her a cup of water, which she examined carefully before drinking.

"Don't worry. It's RV."

"It's what?"

"The water. It's reverse osmosis. No junk in it a'tall."

Her lips twitched and she gulped it down. "Any idea

where I can plug in the truck? Where does Matt plug in his?"

"Matt don't have a truck. He drives a Harley, but not in winter. And Abby ain't usin' her car right now. I'm not sure it's a winter type vehicle, bein' from Texas and all."

"And the Barlow ladies?"

"They don't drive in winter, thank goodness. Lovely women, but Miss Emmaline ain't the greatest driver no more, even in good weather."

"Guess I'll let Sandy figure it out then."

"Yup. I'll come out with you, make sure it starts."

They moved outside into the wind, but before she climbed into the pickup, she turned to Bear. "Listen, I...um..." She hesitantly patted Bear's chest and then rested her hand there, finally able to look him in the eye. "Thank you for what you did in the forest. For listening, for, you know, helping."

"Wouldn't leave you alone with all that on your mind. And I'm here most of the time. Don't be a stranger if you need to talk."

She nodded and hopped into the truck. It started, and she spun gravel and snow driving out onto Bridgeway Avenue.

Bear pursed his lips and shook his head. That Sandy. Bear was sure he'd sent Callie out here for a visit. Well, Bear didn't mind. After Callie's lapse, as she called it, he'd kinda taken on the job of her protector.

Chapter 13

The day of Christmas Eve dawned brilliantly, sun shining, snow glistening.

"The stores close at noon today," Joel told Abby. "If you'd like to go shopping, I can look after Noelle. Or we could all go."

Abby stared at him, her heart filling. She did not deserve the grace he showed her, but not knowing how to handle it, she defaulted to hiding her emotion. "Are you looking for more time with my daughter?"

"With her or with both of you. I would accept either."

Okay then. "I won't be buying any gifts this year, for reasons you already know, but a walk along Main Street might be fun."

"Great. I'll get the stroller ready. There's a breeze, so dress warm, both of you."

"Forget the stroller, Joel. I'll use the wrap today."

Abby enjoyed strolling the beautifully decorated main street, with its lights and Christmas trees and tables of hot chocolate or apple cider to warm them up. With Noelle close to her chest in a snuggly wrap, her hands were free. She let Joel take her hand as they walked and window-shopped or stopped to say hello to people.

"Such a friendly town," Abby said. "It was never this way at home."

"Everyone back home was busy with his own thing. We took each other for granted."

"Do you think so? I've always floated, not wanting to tie myself to anything or anyone."

"I know."

She glanced at him. That's why he called her a butterfly. Flitting from flower to flower, never settling anywhere. There were those years of dating Ricky, but she knew his friends always came before her in his life. Maybe that's why she'd pretended not to care. She never felt that way with Joel, and it was hard to get used to. Did she want to become accustomed to that feeling? She was certainly leaning that way. Could she survive if she learned to depend on someone other than herself, and then he disappeared from her life?

"Let's go back to the hotel," she said. "I want a rest before tonight. It will be a long evening of smiling and trying to stay warm during the Living Nativity."

After a rest and a warm meal of pulled pork, Matt took Joel, Abby and Noelle out to Alkmaar's dairy farm with a truck he'd borrowed from Jerry Alkmaar. When they saw the backdrop for their scene, Abby was immediately entranced by the setup. Straw bales were piled here and there to cut the breeze, and to add to the ambience. A little fence had been strung up to corral Gabby, Cassie and Fiona, who hummed with concern at their new surroundings. Eleanor stayed nearby, helping to set up the scene and to settle her girls.

A couple of cows ate hay in the back of the shed, adding warmth and sound—and aroma—to the event, while their calves came and went freely, at home and near their mothers.

Belvina, whose name Abby had heard around town, arrived to dress Abby and Joel in appropriate robes and head coverings, and to wrap little Noelle in a soft blue blanket. "It's alpaca wool," she said. "A gift from Eleanor."

Abby looked around for the alpaca lady, and called a "thank you" to her.

"You're very welcome," Eleanor said. "It will help Noelle stay warm."

"The only problem with this gig," said Joel when Belvina had finished and moved to another site to do her job there, "is that we can't follow the route to see the whole show."

"We're recording it all." Matt had stopped by to check that all was well. "I asked a couple of my students to follow through from the beginning to catch it all on camera. We'll watch it together on Christmas Day, how about that?"

"That would be perfect for a Christmas afternoon." Abby had relaxed, sitting on a bale, leaning against a fence rail. "It's toasty warm in here with all these animals and I don't even have to remember any lines."

"Just look at the baby once in a while with adoration." Joel sent her a teasing smile.

"I don't have to rehearse that."

People began to arrive, some on horse-drawn wagons, following the route through the various stopping points in town, some bundled up to walk the mile from Happenstance to the dairy. There were a lot of comments such as, "you must be the new couple," and "you're the young folks with the new baby," and "glad to have you in town."

After a couple of hours, the crowd began to dwindle and Matt texted that he'd be by to pick them up shortly.

Belvina returned to gather their outer garments and asked if she could hold the baby. "I love babies," she cooed. "I have a granddaughter, but we don't see her often."

After her recent trauma, Abby leveled a look at Joel, wondering if he thought that was a good idea. He nodded, and as she reluctantly handed Noelle to Belvina, she tried to make conversation. "Do you have a son or a daughter?"

"A daughter first, then twin sons."

"Are they coming home for Christmas?"

Belvina looked unhappy, but eventually gave her a grim smile and shook her head. "Our daughter and her family are out east. Too far to come. And our sons are in Texas, enjoying the sun, apparently. Although, one of the boys is off in Europe somewhere for Christmas."

A fluttery feeling clutched at Abby's heart. "I'm Abby Maguire, by the way. My baby is Noelle, and this is our friend, Joel Pickett."

"Pleased to formally meet you. I'm Belvina. Belvina Rampole. And this is my husband, Bob. Come say hello, Bob."

"Rampole?" Abby stood abruptly, and Joel put his hand on her back. "What are your sons' names, if you don't mind me asking?"

"Oh, of course I don't mind. Ryley and Ricky. Ricky is the one in Europe."

The world began to spin as Abby watched Belvina cuddle Noelle. She looked to Joel, at a loss for words. He leaned in and whispered in her ear. "Are you okay? Do you want me to tell them?"

Dumbly, she nodded, tears spilling from her eyes.

"What's wrong?" asked Belvina. "Would you like to have Noelle back?"

Abby took Noelle and held her close, leaning against Joel for support, and for the words she couldn't produce.

She nodded to Joel, who then asked Belvina and Bob to

sit with them on the bales. He cleared his throat several times before he could get the words out. "First, Bob and Belvina Rampole, Abby and I are not a couple. She needed a friend on this journey, so I rode along. Second, Noelle is not my child. Her biological father is—was—a good friend of mine from college. His name is...Ricky Rampole."

Belvina's hands flew to cover her mouth, but they could not stifle the cry that seemed to come from the depths of her soul. "Ricky's baby? Bob," she grabbed her husband's arm, "Bob, this is Ricky's..."

She didn't finish her sentence, but Abby finished it for her, her words coming out in a sob. "Noelle is your granddaughter."

Belvina's tears ran freely down her cheeks. "Bob." She appealed to her husband for help, then burst into heart-rending sobs. "They never come home," she wailed. "They left us, moved far away, and they never come home. We have only seen our granddaughter once, and she is over two years old. I don't know why they hate us—"

Bob tried to console her. "Shh. Belvina, don't. It doesn't help."

"I can't help it." She gasped her words through tears. "Everyone knows the truth, but we keep pretending it's all fine. The only reason we knew Ricky was in Europe is because he wired for money. And...and now you're here." Her eyes sought Abby's as they shone with a new realization. "This has to be a miracle."

"Yes." Abby repeated the words, swiping at the tears that kept coming. "A Christmas miracle."

Since she had been awake long into the night after the Christmas Eve Pageant, Abby slept in on Christmas Day. The event must have affected Noelle too, as she'd only been awake twice for quick feedings that night. And now it was closing in on 9 a.m.

Abby chugged down the glass of water on her nightstand, then picked up a fussing Noelle, changed her and settled down to feed her. Propped up against the headboard of her bed,

Abby let her thoughts fly back to the shocking news she and Joel had heard. Ricky Rampole was from Happenstance. His parents lived here, and were more than thrilled about Noelle.

Abby wasn't sure how she felt. Surprised to the very soles of her feet, that's for sure. Bob Rampole seemed like a nice guy, but Belvina was a basket case. *Be fair, Abby. How would you feel if you discovered your grandchild had popped up in your town?* The situation was too unexpected to fathom.

The Barlow ladies had been reticent to say much about the Rampoles. "You need to get to know each other and find how it all fits together in your head and heart. They are decent people, but they've faced such heartache when their children left and never returned."

Always a struggle not to judge, thought Abby, and yet, she should know better; she'd been judged more often than not. It was only right that the Rampoles had the chance to create a relationship with their granddaughter. She knew they couldn't help but love little Noelle. They'd had a difficult time letting her go last night.

Joel hadn't said much, but she knew he was madly processing in his way. He had encouraged her to talk it out though, willing to listen, even though repeated talk of Ricky no doubt irritated him. Ricky, the betrayer, the abandoner, the loser.

There I go judging again, she thought. A glance at Noelle reminded her that Ricky was the baby's father, and Abby decided she would not disrespect him to Noelle, "so help me God."

At her whispered words, she thought of Reverend Selig. She needed a good, long talk with him and Annaliese, because she'd need help to keep that promise to herself and to Noelle. Supernatural help. Dare she say it? Spiritual help? She'd made a goal for herself, a far-reaching one. *What's happening to me? I've never taken the time to meditate on anything this far out.*

Maybe that Bible the reverend was talking about would give her some answers. Right now, she needed to burp Noelle and head out to find some breakfast. She was starving. And she'd momentarily forgotten that this was Christmas Day. Abby was positive Johanna would serve an enormous and devastatingly delicious brunch. And Matt had promised a video of the Living Nativity this afternoon.

Also, she needed a distraction from her current introspection. Her butterfly wings were in danger of falling off altogether.

⁂

"Bear has officially hired me to help him at his shop." Joel told Abby the news after a sumptuous Christmas Day brunch. The Barlow sisters had gone for naps, and Matt and Sandy were involved in a competitive game of cards in the parlor. Sandy said Callie was more than happy to spend the day with the Seligs, who had instantly become family to her, seeing she had none of her own.

Abby's silence had Joel wondering if he'd done the right thing, signing on with Bear, but when she finally spoke, he relaxed.

"Joel, are you sure this is what you want? Staying here to watch over me and Noelle?"

"If I didn't care for you, and now your daughter, I would still be back in Texas, or at medical college."

"Or in Europe with..."

"No, Abby. Their trip was an excuse for an extended party and for making bad decisions, and I'm not into that. You have long been at the top of my list. I wouldn't be able to concentrate on my studies if I left you to work all this out on your own."

"But Joel, none of this is your doing. I am facing the outcome of my own actions. I have arranged to have a long talk with Reverend Selig and Annaliese tomorrow to confront my present and my past, not only for me but for Noelle."

He had trouble taking all this in. Finally, half in jest, he said, "Body snatchers."

"Huh?"

"Who are you and what have you done with Abigail Maguire?"

She snorted. "Exactly my thoughts earlier. But you know what? I think I could get to like this new Abigail."

His heart filled as he considered how she was changing and growing as a human being. As an adult with others to take care of. Would there ever be a future for them? He couldn't even go there right now. Just enjoy the present and let God lead. He'd been doing a lot of searching and praying too, and Bear had been a rock. He did have one concern, though. "Abby, don't let anyone clip your wings."

He stood to get more coffee. He would sorely miss this fine fare if he moved out of the hotel.

As if reading his mind, Abby asked the question he'd been waiting for. "Where are you going to live?"

"Don't worry about me. Bear has an old mobile home he's going to let me fix up. Not much to look at, but it does have four walls and a roof. The mobile home park is directly behind his shop. Sol Wuppertal lives there too. He's only been managing the bistro for less than a year."

"Really? I wonder what his story is. Maybe Johanna will have mercy and send along a few leftovers for you from time to time."

"One can always hope." Changing the subject, he said, "What are you going to do about the Rampoles?"

She looked directly at him. "I believe every grandparent should experience having their grandbabies close in order to form attachments and relationships with them. I'm beginning to see what I missed because my parents didn't stay close to extended family. I'm going to get to know Belvina better and let her have access to Noelle. She obviously loves her. The poor woman has been denied the joy of grandparenting, but that changes now." She took a sip of her coffee, then added, "Do you agree?"

"You're asking me?...Oh yeah, you just did!"

"Well?" Her smile was warm.

"I think that is a very wise and kind decision, and I concur totally. There are a lot of people around town who will be keeping their eyes on the situation, if I read Happenstance correctly, and I think Noelle will greatly benefit from this relationship."

She closed her eyes and smiled. "You should know that since you have decided to stay, I will be leaning on you to help me make these decisions, or at least consider them with me. Is that acceptable to you?"

He couldn't help himself. He reached across the table and

took her hands. "Abby, I swear I will do whatever I can to support you and Noelle in this new phase of your life. You know I love her. As to the relationship between you and me, I am willing to let than develop or not, as time goes by. Is that acceptable to you?"

She gave his hand a squeeze and nodded, her eyes tearing up. "Thank you," she whispered. "You are a lifesaver and a true friend."

His heart full, Joel needed fresh air. He had to step back and let the future expand as it would. He released her hands and excused himself. "Remember, you'll always be a butterfly."

Chapter 14

All Christmas afternoon townspeople dropped by the hotel for coffee or hot chocolate and Johanna's delicious *Weinachtskuchen,* and Bear was one of the first. The Christmas goodies tasted even better than they looked, which was saying something.

"You blew that ship right outta the water, Johanna," said Bear as he heaped a second plate full of the confections.

Johanna's blush deepened, and she glanced longingly over her shoulder to her kitchen. Meanwhile, Misses Grayce and Emmaline called for quiet while they presented their personal chef with a long, flat gift box. She set it on the end of the dining table and pulled off the lid, along with the tissue wrap inside. Her gasp carried across the hall to those watching the Living Nativity on screen in the parlor. They paused the show to find out what the fuss was about.

From the box, Johanna gently lifted several items. First was a narrow, personalized cutting board engraved vertically with a logo of a chef's hat above crossed spatulas, and at the bottom, Johanna's name. Next, the box included an apron with signatures of many of the townsfolk, and lastly, a large knife with the words, "Johanna Schmid, Master Chef," etched into the blade.

Johanna's words were few but effective. "Best knife it is, in world." She checked every inch of it, her eyes shining with tears of gratitude. "*Danke sehr!*" she said. "*Danke, danke.*"

"That looks like a deadly weapon," said Sandy, back from his communion with his beloved trees in Lakeview Forest.

The scathing glare he received from Johanna was one that none of the gathered company had ever seen. Sandy immediately stood, both hands held out. "No, no, ma'am. I would never dream of touching your knife." He put his hands to his throat, and Johanna chuckled, while everyone else let out the breath they had held. She slipped the knife back into its sheath and carried it to her kitchen, the word "private" on the door carrying new clout.

Bear, scanning the group, asked Sandy where his

assistant was. "It's Christmas Day, man. Surely you don't have her working out in the cold and snow alone."

"No way," assured Sandy. "She's with the Seligs. I'm sure they'll stop by yet this afternoon."

Later, when Sandy was again caught up in telling another tall tale, the Seligs arrived with Callie in tow. Her eyes roved over the crowd until she caught Bear's eye. She nodded a greeting.

He found his way to her side. "A very merry Christmas to you, Callie."

"Thanks. Same to you."

They shared a bit of banter, which she was not good at, then drifted apart. He looked for her later but she was nowhere to be seen, but he had an idea where she might be.

Slipping away as quietly as he could, he headed down the end hall to the chapel. He knocked on the door with a tentative tap and waited. No answer. Maybe she was sleeping. He tried again, but not a sound within. Was she okay?

He knocked once more and whispered, "I'm stepping in to see if you're alright." With that, he pushed open the door and peeked inside.

Callie lay on one of the few pews, her jacket bunched beneath her head. When the door opened, she lifted her head, revealing a pale, swollen face with dark circles around reddened eyes. Bear wouldn't have recognized her but for the hardware and ink. And her bright red hair, of course.

Her glance up at him was at first angry, then weary. She closed her eyes and lowered her head to the bench. "I can't talk right now." Her voice rasped as if she'd been crying for a while. He hadn't even seen her leave the main rooms, but she must have come here to be alone with her memories.

"Do you need somethin', Callie? If you don't wanna talk, I can just be here so's you're not alone."

No answer.

He settled down at the end of her pew and held out a plate. "Here, you gotta try some of these cookies."

She took one and nibbled, then set it aside. "Can't eat right now, but thanks."

"More for me." He gradually consumed the rest of the treats while she lay quiet.

"You said you got the piercings and tattoos to remember your loved ones. Any other reason?"

Her eyes popped open. "You a psychiatrist now too?"

He ignored her sarcasm. "Nah, not me. Just wonderin' if they were to keep people away."

After a pause, she answered. "Maybe."

"Scare people off?"

"Whatever works. Obviously, it isn't working with you."

He grinned. "Took me a bit, but I'm seein' them as masks to hide behind. Am I right?"

"You wouldn't underst—"

"Try me. I ain't born yesterday. I've heard a thing or two, and I know people. I know when they're hurtin', like you are right now."

Lord, shut up my big mouth! Bear needed to learn to wait, to let people talk when they were ready, 'stead of jumpin' in like that. Now she'd either call him a foul name or slap him upside the head. Most likely both.

But Callie didn't shout or slap. She squeezed her eyes shut, and the tears slipped out. She sat up and tried to speak a couple times, then shook her head and remained quiet, her head resting on her clenched hands.

"Now, listen Callie, you don't know me from Adam, but I'm thinkin' you got a mess of heartbreak that needs unloadin'. Sandy's a good man, but he ain't the best listener."

"And you are?"

"Not the best, but pretty good."

"Why do you want to bother?"

"Cuz you need to share, and I care about you. That's my Christmas gift to you. That's what we do here in Happenstance, we care. The good Lord says we are to share our burdens, so share away, Callie, girl. No judgment from me."

"What do you want to know?"

"Hmm. Let's see. How about telling me what you love and what you hate?"

She composed herself for a minute, then took a deep breath. "All that I have loved lies buried in the past. Literally. Everything makes me angry or sad now."

Not knowing what to say to that, Bear remained silent

while Callie talked.

———————

"We were so young, me and Gabe, but we were in love. Got married right out of college. Did everything together as much as possible. Weren't expecting to have kids right away, but it happened, you know, and we put ourselves into that with whole hearts.

"Benji and Belle were a handful, but sweet as sugar. And daring. Not bad, just busy. And then came Sheera. Such a touch of heaven."

Bear didn't say anything, just sat with his chin in his hand. Callie pushed herself into a sitting position, her feet tucked up on the bench beside her.

"Gabe was such a heart-reader. He knew I was wearing out, so one day he offered to take the kiddos for a ride in the car." She whispered a chuckle. "Whole back seat stuffed with car seats. Gabe buckled them all up and took them for a drive. I was supposed to sleep. But I couldn't. I lay down, but as I was about to drift off, I heard them. They were crying, screaming for me."

She saw her horror reflected on Bear's face. Tears slid down his cheeks but he didn't interrupt.

"It was a drunk driver. Hit them broadside at an intersection. He didn't even get hurt, Bear. Not a scratch. And then he passed out while my babies screamed. I can't get it out of my head. When I heard that baby crying the other day, I took her to protect her. I lost my place in time and was reliving it all. I couldn't even save one of them. And now I'm alone."

"You're not alone, Callie girl. I'm here, and there are many more of us who'll help you through this. Remember what the Seligs said."

"Yeah, well I've gone too far this time. Kidnapping! I did that, Bear. How do you explain that away? I can't leave town, even if I had somewhere to go. I can't be trusted."

He reached over, took her hand and rubbed it with his thumb. With his other hand, he rubbed away his own tears. "You ever heard of PTSD, Callie?"

"Like soldiers get in the war? Of course."

"There's other things that bring on PTSD. Like traumatic

events."

"This isn't like war, Bear. Everybody experiences trauma at times. I'm a poorly-adjusted woman who went off the deep end. No excuses."

Bear was silent, but kept rubbing Callie's hand, and she felt her heartbeat slow to normal. No one could excuse what she'd done.

"You just gave me the exact explanation of the situation. You got yourself a trauma, you got yourself depression and shuttin' yourself off from anyone who wants to get close. You pretend you don't care about anything or anyone so's you don't have to feel."

The words hit deep and hard. He was right. She knew it. She'd never thought of herself as suffering as much as a soldier. But she was traumatized, for sure. And alone, and protecting herself the best she could. "What can I do?"

Bear slid over on the pew and put his arms around her. He felt like a shelter, like a solid place that kept her from falling further down, if there were any further for her to fall. She held on for dear life.

They sat that way for what seemed like hours, until she came to herself. "Bear, we have to get out of here. What will people think?"

"Don't matter what anybody thinks. We know what happened here, and it needed time." He tilted his head to catch her eyes. "You ready to leave this sanctuary?"

She chuckled, thinking how the sanctuary was Bear's firm embrace more than any room they were in. With a sigh that came from her soul, she let go of him, sat up and rubbed her eyes. "I must look a mess."

He raised his brows at her.

"Okay, then. Doesn't matter what others think. Anyway, I need to go back to the Seligs'. I hope I haven't kept them waiting for me."

"If they've gone, I'll run you over there in my truck."

She gave him her best smile and stood to go. His hand on her shoulder gave her the courage she needed to face the world again. The best Christmas gift she'd received in a long, long while.

After all the company on Christmas Day, Abby set to work picking up in the parlor and fluffing pillows.

"Oh, my dear," said Emmaline, stopping at the doorway, "you are our guest. You don't need to do that."

"It's the least I can do," said Abby. "You've given me a comfortable room and unbelievable food, as well as friendship."

"Yes, well, our Johanna can't help herself. She is perfection in the kitchen."

"Please let me help a bit. I'm getting bored sitting around being catered to. And Noelle is sleeping—"

"—like a baby!" laughed Emmaline. "She is a good baby. If you're content to help pick up, I will go have a wee nap. Yesterday was rather draining."

Abby couldn't believe how her life had changed, how it was coming together day by day. Who would have guessed she would be a mother? She moved to the sunroom by the front doors and tidied up there. Hearing a vehicle, she glanced out one of the long windows to see if she could recognize the car. It was a recent model in silver-gray, and it looked about to park, when the driver turned the car around and left.

Abby's first reaction was fear. Was Callie stalking her and Noelle? Surely not. The woman had apologized profusely and Abby had finally accepted that, on the terms that Callie not come to the hotel alone. Abby found Grayce behind the counter of the hotel entrance, and asked her who drove a car like that.

"That would be Belvina Rampole."

Hmm. Maybe it was time to visit Belvina, figure out some sort of regular visiting time.

When Abby had cleaned up, she called Belvina and invited her for coffee.

"Where? At the bistro?"

"No, Belvina. Here, at the hotel. I have a feeling there are leftovers from yesterday."

"Oh. Okay. Are you sure?"

"Absolutely. Noelle has been missing you."

"How...I will be there in half an hour."

When Belvina showed up, Abby was ready for her. Noelle was fed, changed, and down for another nap. A plate of delectables waited on the dining table, and the moment they moved to sit down, Johanna served coffee.

Belvina looked left and right, peering as far into the kitchen as possible. She chuckled sheepishly and sat. "I have an inquisitive mind," she said.

Abby had heard it referred to in different terms, but she thought this admission was already surprising. "Let's move across to the parlor. It's just the two of us for coffee today, so we can talk freely."

"Lovely cookies," said Belvina, "but then I guess you didn't bake them yourself."

Hmm. Not big on tact.

"I've never had to do much on my own, but I did work in a restaurant for about a year before I came up here."

"I don't do a lot of cooking or baking anymore," said Belvina, "but I know how. You and Noelle will have to stop by, maybe once a week, and I'll teach you what I know."

Her offer didn't surprise Abby, but helped her realize how lonely this woman was. "That will also give us a chance to get out once in a while. Thank you. I'll accept anything you can teach me."

Abby heard Noelle stirring and squirming on the monitor. She excused herself to pick her up from her nap. When she returned, Belvina was quietly weeping.

"What's the matter, Belvina? What can I do for you? How can I help you over your hurt?"

"Oh dear. I'm sorry. I can't seem to stop my tears. Or my emotion."

"Of course. We've all been through a traumatic discovery. I want you to know you are always welcome to spend time with your granddaughter. Okay?"

Belvina's brimming eyes looked up into Abby's. "Really? I'm not well-liked around town, you know. Too nosy, people say."

"People don't know the whole story, though, do they? They don't know the pain you try to cover, the loneliness you suffer."

"Why are you being kind to me, Abby? My son hurt you, and your baby. He deserves to deal with the consequences, but I don't know if he even has emotions. How did you get involved with him, anyway?"

Abby took a deep breath and blew it out, ready to face the future. "First of all, Belvina, I have made a decision which, if you are going to be spending time with my daughter, you must agree to."

Her head came up, and Abby noted the fear in her eyes. She hurried to comfort her with a hand on her arm. "Nothing too difficult...well, it could be, but we can do it."

"What is it? Just tell me and I will try."

"Although Noelle will never know your son as a father figure, you and I must remember that she will know of her origins when she is old enough to understand, and we must not ruin her opinion of him. He doesn't know what he's given up, but he may one day. Whatever the case, if and when we speak of Ricky, we will maintain respect for him as her biological father. Can we be in agreement about that?"

Belvina's eyes seemed to drill through her. "Oh. Well. It will take some practice, and you will have to help me until it becomes a habit. I'll tell Bob; he's good at reminding me of things."

"Thank you. That's all I can ask."

"Do you..." Belvina hesitated, her face growing pink, then tried again. "Do you think you and Ricky would ever...you know..."

Abby's head was shaking even before she finished speaking. "I'm sorry, Belvina, but I will not trust him again, and he will not be part of Noelle's life. There may be someone else one day, but never Ricky. Can you accept that?"

"Accept it? I'm thankful. Noelle deserves better than that. Oh dear, that's a negative comment again, isn't it? I do love him as only a mother can, but I understand Ricky has proven himself untrustworthy as a partner. Better?"

Abby leaned over and kissed Belvina's cheek, then sat down to enjoy a cup of coffee with the woman who would never be her mother-in-law, but would hopefully be a cherished grandmother to Noelle. Belvina cuddled the baby against her chest. Time would heal, Abby mused, and Noelle would be a gigantic part of that healing.

———————

Since Bear had given him a couple hours off that afternoon—"Gotta wait for them parts to come"—Joel asked Abby to meet him at the bistro.

"I'm glad you called," said Abby, pulling Noelle from her carrier and handing her to Joel. "I think she's been missing you while you're at work."

His heart soared as he took Noelle in his arms. "Hey, little girl, how are you doing these days? Is your mom managing okay?" He winked at Abby, who tried to pretend she hadn't seen. Then she grinned.

"We're fine, thank you very much. I'm treated like a star at the hotel, but I've been doing my best to help in small ways. When there's major cleaning to do, the ladies call in Leah Wuppertal. She's a sweet girl, and she loves Noelle too."

Sol stopped by to deliver their coffees and a snack, and they visited with him for a few minutes. "Coffee time is about over for today," he said. "I have time to say hi." He turned to Joel. "I hear Bear is fixing up one of the mobile homes for you. I hope you're not too fussy. Those units should be condemned."

"As long as there are no rats, I can handle it."

"Mice okay, then?"

"Stop, you two." Abby looked a bit queasy. "I hate mice."

Another customer entered the bistro and Sol excused himself. Joel wanted to know what else was new for the girls. "Any ideas for the future?"

Abby laughed. "Remember when I used to get mad at you for asking about the future? I've sure had to eat my words. Noelle is the future, and I need to keep that in mind."

"Whoever you are, you are definitely impersonating Abby."

Her laugh warmed his soul. "Joel, you'll never guess who I invited for coffee yesterday."

He waited, then realized he'd have to guess. "Let's see. I don't know."

"Noelle, give him a hint."

He looked at Abby. "You're kidding! Not Belvina."

"Yup. I saw her drive up to the hotel, then turn around and drive away. I think she's lonely. I asked her over and she was there in no time. She's been deeply hurt by her kids. I told her she's always welcome to see her granddaughter. She cried and we talked about...all kinds of things."

"You talk about Ricky?"

Abby paused before she answered. "Actually, yes. First, I had to convince her that Ricky would never be part of our lives, although Noelle would know who her father is. Second, I have made a decision not to bad-mouth him in front of his daughter, starting now, and I needed Belvina to agree to the same."

"I'll bet that's going to be tough on her."

"Yeah, she said that too, but she's willing to try. She loves her son, as only a mother could, she said, but she doesn't want him involved in Noelle's life."

"Is that good with you?"

"What do you mean?"

"I mean do you ever, you know, think of Ricky?"

Abby reached over and covered his hand with her own. "Only when I look at Noelle's coloring, her dark hair. But he's not in my heart, never was. I didn't have boundaries back then, but I'm drawing them a lot more lately."

Joel was glad he had asked, even though he wasn't sure he could handle her answer, had it been different. With Ricky out of the picture now and later, he felt freer to hope that a relationship with Abby might be possible.

"Joel," she interrupted his thoughts, "don't worry. I have a feeling things are going to work out for the best. That's what the reverend says. He says the best prayer to ask is that God's will be done. How about them apples?"

"You amaze me, Abigail."

"I amaze myself sometimes." She giggled, and although she pulled her hand away from his, he saw reluctance in her eyes. And maybe even hope. This sudden arrival in Happenstance was not a coincidence by any stretch of the imagination.

Chapter 15

"Good morning. May I please speak with Miss Abigail Maguire?"

Abby clicked her phone to speaker and set it on the dresser while she finished changing Noelle. "This is Abby. Who's calling?"

"My name is Aristotle Philatopoulos—Phil for short. We haven't met, but I run the Waldorf café next door to Sol's bistro. Perhaps you've heard my name mentioned as the new owner of the Orchard Grove Restaurant as well?"

"Isn't that the old building near the golf course? Maisie toured me around town."

"One and the same. I am resurrecting the restaurant, and would appreciate additional time for this project, but the Waldorf still has regular customers who deserve my attention. I hear you may be interested in a part-time job; that's why I'm calling. I need someone to manage the Waldorf in the mornings while I spend time at the Orchard Grove. Would you have any interest in my proposal?"

Abby had to stop and think. Who had given Phil her name? Who knew she wouldn't mind some work, both for a change of pace, and to earn some money to live on?

"Hello, are you still on the line, Abigail?"

"Oh yes, I'm sorry. You caught me by surprise. I might very well be interested in your offer. Are you able to tell me who gave you my name?"

"She didn't say not to, so I believe I may share that information. It was Belvina Rampole."

"Really! Interesting." She thought for a moment. "I'd have to arrange for babysitting. I have a little girl now."

"I've heard. A beautiful child, says Mrs. Rampole. She said she might be able to assist you with babysitting, but she had yet to discuss that with you."

Belvina offered to babysit? Without asking me? Well, no. She implied to Phil that she would talk with me about it. "Yes, Phil? If you'd give me a few days, I'll see what I can do about babysitting for Noelle, and I'd also like to drop by the Waldorf to get a handle on what is all involved. I've been a server before, but never in charge."

"I would most certainly train you. My reputation is on the line."

"All right. I'll get back to you in a few days, say, by the weekend. Is that okay?"

"Of course. There is no particular rush, but when Mrs. Rampole suggested you, the idea seemed excellent to me. I will await your call or visit."

Abby hung up the phone, only to be startled by its ringing as soon as she did. "Hello?"

"Hello, Abby? This is Belvina calling. Am I catching you at a bad time?"

"No, not at all. I just had a very interesting conversation with Phil from the Waldorf."

"Oh dear. I wanted to talk to you before he did. I don't want you to think I'm trying to manipulate you. I'm sorry about that."

Wow, an apology, just like that. This would take some getting used to. "No worries. Phil said you'd be calling."

"And? What do you think of my idea? Does it suit you? Would you trust me to look after Noelle for a few hours each day?"

"Of course I would, Grandma. We'd have to figure out a few things, such as what you'd need at your house, but those are details. I said I'd get back to Phil by the weekend."

"What will you tell him?"

"That I'll take him up on his offer if he gives me some leeway. I'll have to have someone to cover for me when Noelle needs nursing."

Belvina was silent so long, Abby wondered if she'd hung up. Then she spoke. "I don't know if I should mention this. I don't want to frighten you off or anything. But I could be a nanny of sorts."

"If I had my own home, I'd welcome that, but right now, I can't agree to something that involves the Barlow sisters and their hotel."

"I understand. That's why I'm wondering if you'd be at all interested in staying here"—she cleared her throat— "living here, I mean. With Bob and me. You'd be free to come and go as you need to, never worrying about Noelle. We have lots of room. You could have the whole upstairs, which includes a kitchenette."

Abby could hardly speak. "Why are you being nice to me? You hardly know me, and my past actions are questionable."

"We all have pasts, Abby. A whole new world has opened up to me over the past few days, a world of color and depth and meaning. And Bob needs more too. He doesn't talk much, but he is definitely drawn to Noelle as I am. We need you and Noelle as much, if not more, than you need us."

Wiping her eyes with her fingers, Abby sniffled. "It's a deal, Grandma!"

Abby had to blow her nose when she hung up. She was sure Belvina had the same teary smile on her face that she herself wore.

"Joel!" Abby's greeting put him on guard as soon as he heard her voice over the phone. Was she in some trouble? Or was something up with Noelle?

"Abby, is everything okay?"

"Yes, absolutely. Sorry if my excitement sounded like panic."

"Okay then. Let me sit down and recover."

"Was it a long day at Bear's?"

Her concern touched him. "Don't worry about my day. It's a hoot working for Bear, and I'm learning a lot too. But, yeah, I've been on an extended vacation since we left Texas, and I'm not used to regular hours."

"Any news on the mobile home?"

"Oh, Abby. Those places should be hauled away and buried. Sol's place is okay; he gave me a tour last night, but it's the best of the lot, next to Bear's. I think I'll be looking for something—anything—else."

"Bummer. I'll keep my ears open for something. Maybe the reverend and Annaliese would pray about it. They seem to get answers."

"You sure I don't have the wrong number? Is this Abby?"

Her chuckle revived him, bringing on a big smile. She sounded like she was flourishing here in Happenstance.

Who'da thought! "What's the big news that has you all excited? You've been patiently waiting to tell me."

"Yes! Listen to this. Belvina suggested to Phil that I might be willing to work for him at the Waldorf. Part-time. And she offered to babysit. Not only that, she said they had tons of room in their house, like the whole upstairs, which has a mini-kitchen, and we could stay there and she would be a built-in nanny."

He was quiet for a few moments. "You're kidding! Did you win a lottery or what?" He had almost lost faith in happy endings. This was over the top. "Abby, this is perfect. Do you think you're ready for work? As in, are you back to enough strength to be on your feet all day?"

"Of course I am. And Phil was talking about mornings for now. Actually, I've been taking Noelle for stroller walks every day, or going myself if she's asleep and the sisters are both home. I'm ready for the next step. I'm starting to get bored. Phil needs to get some work done on his other restaurant."

"He has another restaurant? Here in town?"

"Yeah, the Orchard Grove. It's an old dining place with a horsehair dance floor that he's resurrecting, as he calls it. The Barlows were telling me about it. It's down by the golf course. I'll show you sometime if you'd like to go for a drive."

Joel was liking the sound of this more and more. Abby was treating him like a good friend, not someone who was out to manage her. And not an occasional friend. He could get used to this. He was very glad he had decided to stay in town. "I have some news of my own."

"Tell all!"

He'd love to tell her his heart, but she wasn't quite ready to hear it. Must go slowly. "I got a call too. From Dr. Paula. She wants me to go with her to Athens one day a week to volunteer at her crisis clinic there."

"Whoa. What would be expected of you there?"

"Whatever needs doing, I guess. She says it's on-the-job training. I still have to run it past Bear."

"Did you tell her about your dreams of becoming a doctor—"

"Stop what you're saying. I know what's next. A deferral was my decision, Abby. And yes, I did. I met her at Hanson's

Market and we chatted for a while. Her dad used to run the clinic, while she was a cop and then studying to be a doctor, but he wants to—needs to—retire. He already takes lots of fishing trips."

"How did we end up here, Joel? In this place of second chances? It certainly wasn't happenstance."

He laughed. "I agree. I'm getting excited about what's coming next. Wouldn't miss this for the world."

"Then I guess I did you a favor, huh?"

If you only knew. "You betcha, Abby." He cleared his throat and willed his voice not to wobble. "Thanks for letting me know your news. We need to take some time to swap stories."

Her voice softened. "Yes, we do. 'Nite, Joel."

Chapter 16

"You look different." Callie sent Bear a half-smile when they met at the Waldorf Café.

"Got me a new shirt, over to Wuppertal's."

Her smile widened. "It's more than the shirt, Bear. You look...jaunty."

His eyebrows drew down. "Is that good?"

"It's great. Tell me why you wanted to meet at the Waldorf instead of Sol's bistro."

He pulled open the door of the café and ushered her in ahead of him. Only two other customers nursed their coffees behind newspapers in the back booth. "No nosy neighbors."

"Ah. Thanks for thinking of that. Word spreads and mothers with children will turn tail and run."

"Callie. No more of that, now."

She mashed her lips together, the mere memory of her huge faux pas filling her with remorse and embarrassment. She'd have to get used to forgiveness. It was the forgiving of herself that evaded her.

They sat, and Phil brought them coffees and the mincemeat tarts Bear had pointed out when they entered.

"I haven't had mincemeat since I was a kid." Callie savored the taste, along with the nostalgia. "So good."

Bear had consumed two already. She figured she'd better dig in too, if she wanted any.

"Does it bother you that they call you Bear?"

"No, not a'tall. It's my Happenstance name, you know, and I been here for many years. My people are from here now, and that's their preferred name. I like it."

"Do you mind if I call you Gavin?"

"Don't mind a'tall, nope. It will be a treat. No one calls me that 'cept the Barlows, and my dear mama always did too." He grinned and reached for another tart. "Sorry. Big appetite." He popped the confection into his mouth, chewed a couple times and swallowed.

Callie hid her grin in a swig of coffee. "This is good coffee."

"Yes, it is. The bistro has fancy stuff, and very tasty, but Phil has always made a good cup of coffee. 'Course, Joel would ask me how I know that, seein' as I have deadened my taste buds on my shop sludge." He sat back as he took another swig, then leveled her a look. "One for one. What is your real name? I know it's Callie and not Cal, but what else?"

Callie had to remind herself she didn't have to hide anymore, but it was a tough uphill struggle. She cleared her throat and mumbled, "Callista Victoria Cornwallis Simonson."

Bear choked on his coffee. When he'd got himself together, he said, "Say what?"

She heaved a frustrated sigh. The name made her feel like a socialite, which she most definitely was not. "Callista Victoria. My maiden name was Cornwallis, and my married name is Simonson."

"That's quite the handle for such a little lady."

"Not much of a lady." She hung her head and wiped at a spot on the table.

Bear reached out and lifted her chin. "You are a lady, Callie, and a very special one. Keep your chin up, okay?"

She blinked to keep back the stupid tears and nodded.

"Now, how are the meetings with the psychoanalyst, or whatever you call her?"

Taking a deep breath, she steadied, and reminded herself this was Bear—Gavin—she was talking to. "Going well, Gavin. She keeps pushing me to remember more and look at it realistically. It helps to push off some of the guilt, but it wears me out to relive that time."

She waited for him to say that nothing that had happened in the past was her fault, but he didn't. He focused on her and listened. Wow. What a guy. She told him about her most recent appointment, and they discussed what was coming next. The visit with Gavin was as effective in settling her nerves as the counseling sessions. He had a unique way of making her comfortable with him and with herself.

When she was done telling, he said, "Have you talked with Abby? Or Joel?"

"Yeah. Just a bit. They are both very forgiving, but I think they're still hesitant because this PTSD is not easily controlled. I think it will always be a thing for me."

Bear nodded, sorrow in his eyes. "I hate that you had to go through all that. And alone. Where were your supporters?"

"I've wondered that too. Gabe's family was too overwhelmed to help anyone else. They kind of cut me loose. My folks had passed already. No relatives bothered to come forward."

"People can sure let you down. But I'm here, Callie. I have come forward. And I ain't steppin' back. I want to help you regain as much of yourself as you can."

This time the tears spilled. "I don't know why you are so good to me. You hardly know me."

"But I'm lookin' forward to gettin' to know you better, Callie girl. If you don't mind, that is."

Smiling through her tears, Callie said, "Gavin, there's nothing that would make me happier than getting to know you better. You have been a rock, and I'll need help to get through this."

"Then I'm your man."

Phil came up at that moment with a coffee refill, and both Bear and Callie reddened.

"I didn't mean nothin' by that comment, Phil. She...we're just friends..." He waved a hand. "Never mind."

"Yes, I agree this is lovely December weather. I do believe the Living Nativity will become an annual event, don't you?"

Bear and Callie both nodded enthusiastically, then giggled once Phil left.

"I have to go help Sandy with some more forest evaluation," said Callie, "but I would love to have coffee here with you again."

"Said and done." He moved out of his seat, then offered Callie his hand. "My lady?"

She threaded her arm through his as they walked out of the café, nearly running over Leah Wuppertal as she rushed over to the bistro with a box of baking. Bear steadied her box and opened the door of the bistro for her. "Guess I better look where I'm goin'."

Bear watched Joel working under the hood of the

Barlows' old car. He knew they'd never get a new vehicle, and made sure it would be safe to drive until it could no longer be fixed. Most probably they'd quit driving if this one gave out. They were still competent to motor around Happenstance, but he didn't like to see them cross the bridge onto the #15 anymore. Grayce wasn't as quick on the draw as she had been, and Emmaline was easily distracted. But that was life. He'd do his best to keep their vehicle roadworthy.

"Hey Pickett," he called.

Joel lifted his head from the motor and waited.

"Coffee time, kid."

With a smirk, Joel wiped his hands on a rag tucked into his back pocket and headed toward Bear's office.

"Grab a chair. Take a load off."

Joel took one of the new-to-you vinyl chairs and sat, one ankle crossed over the other knee.

"You look good with a little grease around the gills," said Bear. "That thing comin' along?"

"Yup. I'll have it done by tonight. Ready for spring, when it comes."

"Good to hear. I can't believe how fast that new coffee machine is. You say you found it at the second-hand shop?"

"Yeah, and I gave it a good cleanup. Some vinegar and a lot of rinsing and it's in fine shape. I put the old coffee maker with the others in the bin around the back of the building. You've got half a dozen of them, Bear."

"Don't wanna talk about it."

Joel snickered. "Coffee's a lot better, right?"

"Yeah, yeah. Don't get all proud now." He liked this kid. He'd be all right.

"You been out with Callie again?"

"What do you mean, again? We had a coffee at Phil's is all."

"Yeah, right. And nearly ran over other pedestrians on your way out, according to word on the street."

"You keepin' track of me?"

"No. I have better things to do. Just saying. By the way, can I ask you something?"

"Course. Just call me the fountain pen of wisdom."

"Dr. Paula asked if I'd be willing to volunteer at her crisis

129

clinic in Athens once a week. Do you think that would work, and if it does, which day would be best?"

"Crisis clinic. Like a medical doctor kind of thing? Emergency stuff? You like that kind of work?"

"I had plans to study medicine, as you probably know, but I put it off until I know Abby and Noelle are okay, or until...well, I'll see what the future holds."

"Just weird, you know, sittin' here, visitin' with a guy who's that kinda smart!" Life was full of surprises. Joel looked like your ordinary kid.

"Let's just say I have an affinity for that kind of thing. I volunteered down in Texas too. If it works out someday, that would be awesome. For now, I'm happy pulling wrenches."

"Huh." He poured coffee for both of them in clean—he looked again in amazement—clean ceramic mugs, and handed one to Joel. "Well, kid, don't let me stand in the way of your learnin'. Gotta get you properly trained so's I can come to you when I get old...older."

Joel was silent a moment, then said, "Another question. Why are so many people in town being good to us? What's the deal?"

Bear chugged the rest of his coffee. "We take care of our own, kid."

"But we're not even from here."

"You crossed the bridge, didn't ya? You belong here now."

"I'm sorry, I'm overstaying my welcome." Joel sat down to breakfast with the Barlow sisters and Matt, about a week after Christmas. "The mobile homes Bear talked about are unlivable."

"And surely unsanitary," added Emmaline. "Mice and dirt and who knows what else?"

"Now that I'm working for Bear, I'd like to pay the usual rent. And if there's anything I can do to help at the hotel, I'd be happy to pitch in."

Matt took a drink of his coffee, then turned his attention to Joel. "I ended up doing the same. My contribution is to keep the business end up and going. I do the books and answer the correspondence...all in cooperation with Miss Grayce and

Miss Emmaline, of course."

"And a fine job he does for us," said Emmaline, "doesn't he, Grayce?"

"I concur completely," said her sister.

Matt took a bite of his egg, then pointed at Joel with his fork. "You know, when the snow goes, there's a lot of outdoor work to do around here. The ladies used to employ a gardener, but he's, what? About 86 years old now?"

"His age is not the factor." Grayce dabbed her mouth with her napkin. "The point is, the poor man is no longer flexible or strong enough to keep up the work, and we certainly don't want him up on a ladder."

Joel's eyes darted from one speaker to another, putting together the possibilities. "I'm sure I could be of service to you outdoors. Even now, I can make sure the paths and steps are free of snow and ice, and once the grass is green again, there will be mowing to do. And some of the trees could use pruning. I have also helped my mother plant dozens of flowers when I lived at home, so I have some experience."

The sisters turned their eyes on each other, sharing a silent message. Then, Emmaline said, "My goodness, yes," and nodded to Joel. "That would work well. Thank you for your offer. This hotel has been our home all our lives, and the longer we can stay right here, the better off we will be."

"Yes," continued Grayce. "Matt's suggestion for us to move to the main floor has greatly relieved our increasing challenges with the long stairway to the upstairs. But there is one sacrifice we might ask you to make now and then."

"Anything." Joel's heart sped up at his agreement, wondering what he had promised.

"We still plan to renovate the conservatory, as well as the rooms on the second and third floors, therefore, you may be asked to gather your things and relocate from time to time. Would that work for you?"

"No problem there." Joel figured a move would take him about ten minutes, since he had brought very little with him, and owned no furniture.

"One more thing." Emmaline raised her hand to snag everyone's attention. "We would like to propose that between you two young men, you would oversee the transformation of the tunnels below stairs. Matthew, you have been in touch with the experts in that field. You can bring Joel up to speed. Is that agreeable?"

"Up to speed, indeed," murmured Grayce. "I would appreciate a moment to consider this, since I have not yet been consulted." Miss Grayce gave her sister a scathing look, then lifted her chin and spoke to the men. "If you are willing, we will include this in your contract, Joel, and add it to yours, Matthew."

"I didn't know I had a cont..." Matt's remark stopped mid-sentence at another of Miss Grayce's stares. Joel noticed and covered a snicker.

"I'd be happy to sign a contract such as this," said Joel. "I can't thank you enough for the opportunity to remain here. Wow. And the meals!"

Miss Emmaline nodded, a wide smile lighting her face. "Johanna will be happy you are staying. Someone else to cook for. And make sure you invite your—our Abby and her little Noelle as often as you wish, once they have moved."

The joy in Joel's heart soared as he considered the future. Happenstance had been non-existent to him only a few weeks ago, and already it was home. He could hardly wait to tell Abby. His Abby? Not yet, but he had hope.

Abby was thrilled that Joel would be able to stay at the hotel for the foreseeable future. What a relief. The walk or bike ride to Bear's shop was a few minutes, and he'd be living in a clean place, well-fed and with more than enough upkeep chores to keep him busy.

As they sat in the parlor, sharing a loveseat, Joel's voice interrupted her thoughts. "Will that be too close to you, Abby? Do we need some space between us for the time being?"

"First of all, we've seen each other nearly every day for four years. Why would we not continue? Especially if..." She stopped, unsure of how to speak her feelings. She was unused to sharing her real heart, didn't even admit it to herself in many cases. But her constant dancing away from life was over. She had already grown roots in this amazing little town. Who knew Happenstance would embrace her like this? Ever since the sizzle she felt crossing the bridge into town in the middle of a blizzard, she hadn't wanted to leave. Not if she were honest with herself. And that's what she wanted to be.

Meanwhile, Joel waited, not filling the silence that followed her unfinished sentence. Okay, she'd get on with it.

"And secondly, I'll be moving to the Rampoles' any day now. Bob and Belvina are packing up their kids' junk and cleaning up before we move. Besides that, I've come to trust you, Joel. I can't imagine not having you around—and not as a temporary convenience! You are the truest friend I've ever had, and the best father-figure Noelle could hope for. If you're willing to be patient with me, I'd like to learn to know you better in a more personal way."

Joel was trying to read her mind, she could tell.

"I'd like that, Abby. I want to be here for you each step of the way, but I don't want to push. You've been changing from the flighty person you were to the responsible and more approachable woman you are."

He took her hand in his and held her eyes. "I can't promise you a perfect life, or one without bumps and obstacles, but if you're willing to go step by step with me, I am certain we can make our relationship work."

Abby knew there was more. "What else, Joel? Let's talk about it now."

"Someday, Abby, I want to marry you. I want to formally adopt Noelle so she is mine, just the way I feel she already is. That's what I wasn't saying."

Abby sat back and folded her arms. "Hmm. Forthright. What if it doesn't work out?"

"I think it's called commitment. That's part of the journey, and I'd say we're in a perfect place to figure it out."

She broke into a grin and clasped both his hands. "Then let's get on with it. One step at a time."

They stood, each noting the time, things to do, people to see. Then she stepped forward and kissed his cheek. "To the journey."

He squeezed her hands, his smile wide and spreading to his eyes. "To the journey."

THE END

Reader's Guide Discussion Questions

1. What was Abby's initial view of elderly people? Did her assessment change over the course of the story?

2. What do you think of Joel's statement: "That's what integrity is about. Doing the right thing even when no one is watching you."

3. Up to this point, Joel's experience with religion is more guilt than glory. How does he reconcile his feelings with the truth he knows?

4. What does Bear mean when he suggests that life is like driving a car in the dark; you can only go as far as the lights shine?

5. How is life like a choose-your-own-ending book?

6. What do you think of Abby's ideas: Sometimes the realities of life are harder when you choose to face them, but the joys of accomplishing new things and taking life in hand is worth it.

7. How can you trust in God when bad things happen?

8. Did Abby deserve the grace shown her? Did Callie? How do you interpret grace?

NOTE: Just for your interest, there is a horsehair dance floor in a neighboring village to where I live. It's called Manitou Beach Danceland, in the tiny hamlet of Manitou Beach, Saskatchewan.

See: https://www.youtube.com/watch?v=qZLDNuznf6c

About the Author

Photo Credit: Dennis Dick

Janice L. Dick is an award-winning author from the Canadian prairies. She has written six historical novels and four contemporary cozy mysteries, as well as short stories, blogs, articles and book reviews. She is the winner of the 2016 Janette Oke Award.

Check out Janice's blog/website: www.janicedick.com
and her Amazon Author page:
https://amazon.com/author/janicedick

Other Books by Janice L. Dick

THE STORM SERIES

Calm Before the Storm

Eye of the Storm

Out of the Storm

IN SEARCH OF FREEDOM SERIES

Other Side of the River

In a Foreign Land

Far Side of the Sea

HAPPENSTANCE CHRONICLES

The Road to Happenstance

Crazy About Maisie

Gossip & Grace

Secrets & Second Chances

SHORT STORIES

The Christmas Sweater

ANTHOLOGIES

Hope is Born: A Mosaic Christmas Anthology

Note From the Author

I have so enjoyed writing these Happenstance books over the years. As old and new characters take the stage in each new novel, I learn more about others and myself.

Many thanks to all those who have supported me in my writing career, among them, my dear friends at Writersink. From first idea to back cover copy, you've been with me, listening, encouraging and critiquing. Thank you.

A big thanks to those who agreed to beta-read and offer comments: Loretta Polischuk, Eleanor Bertin, Janet Sketchley, and others along the way.

I thank Wayne, my husband and best friend, for believing in and encouraging me.

Most of all, thank you to my Lord Jesus Christ for giving me this love of words and story, and for His faithful guidance and love throughout my life. I am His, and He is mine.

I hope and pray that *Secrets & Second Chances*, as told through the eyes of the characters, offers glimpses of the God who loves us more than we'll ever know. I pray for each one of you, that you will experience joy and hope through my stories, and that you will allow the glimpses of glory to bring wholeness into your lives.

See you in the next Happenstance book.
Jan Dick

Let's Connect

Thanks for taking the time to read this story. The nicest thing you can ever do for an author, besides reading his or her books, is to write a brief review and post it on social media, as well as on Amazon.

Oh, and one more thing. If you drop by my website, http://www.janicedick.com/ you will see my newsletter sign-up form. If you take a moment to fill in your name and email, you will receive a concise newsletter from me about once a month. It will include news about my writing and a brief personal note. I'd love to have you on board.